MAKING WAVES

MAKING WAVES

short stories by

Russ Desaulnier

LUMINARE PRESS
WWW.LUMINAREPRESS.COM

MAKING WAVES
Copyright © 2021 by Russ Desaulnier

Printed in the United States of America

Luminare Press
442 Charnelton St.
Eugene, OR 97401
www.luminarepress.com

LCCN: 2021922594
ISBN: 978-1-64388-858-3

For Bonnie
and
Uncle Ted

De gustibus non est disputandum

CONTENTS

The Summer of Love

ometimes they were missing faces, genitals, or legs.
Scheduling from above never kept her in the severe
trauma ward for long stretches, circulating the nurses
for sanity's sake through the other wards of the U.S. Army
Presidio hospital. It was 1967 and the so-called *summer of
love* in San Francisco, and the Haight was overflowing with
stoned-out kids, and all sorts of the curious come to join
the party, while in Vietnam they were mincing flesh in the
jungles and keeping nurses like Jody busy.

Luke used to meet her at a bar near the Presidio com-
pound around five in the afternoon for drinks and com-
miseration. She was a tiny blond with an attractive face but
lined and worn. Luke was desperately looking for work, any
work that would get him started with a regular paycheck.
They met at Sessions Bar one afternoon and that's where
they kept meeting. There was nothing between them. They
were just two people who needed to debrief after a day on
the job, his looking for one and her trying to keep sane after
seeing too much at the hospital.

He was working the agencies and filling out dozens of
forms at a dozen different employment agencies. Ironically,
the MA and 2-S deferments had got him through college
and kept him out of Jody's wards. But there he was past the
draftable age, overeducated, and looking for a starter posi-

tion in just about anything. Fortunately, he had a place to stay while he was trying to find his way. Major Terry Rooney attached to the Presidio was a distant relative of a distant relative who gave him a spare bedroom in Tiburon across the bay. Of course, it had a shelf date, but he was confident something would turn up. The Major told him not to worry because the bedroom wasn't being used. Luke rarely saw the Major except on the weekends, and one Saturday night he invited Luke to relax a bit and join him for drinks in Sausalito, the Major's treat.

Jody also lived over in Tiburon, several apartment complexes away along the main road. Every complex had its own pool and quad where professional singles congregated on weekends. They partied and drank, a distinct set from those who filled the streets in the city, no rags or long hair. Tiburon complexes housed San Francisco's young professionals on their way up.

After two weeks of their meeting at the bar, Jody gave him her apartment address in Tiburon that she shared with another nurse. Jody bought him fifty-cent glasses of beer while she drank Margaritas. She told Luke he could pay her back once he got a job. She was thankful for his company. To be honest, she said, she was glad to have a few drinks with a guy who was whole, and nice, with whom there was no agenda. She was thirty-four, divorced six years prior and saving up to buy a house in Napa. She didn't smoke and every time Luke lit up, she'd warned him about continuing the habit.

He told her he was feeling the pressure of so much rejection by employers and needed a break. Jody responded by inviting him to a Chinese banquet being given by one of the head physicians she worked under at the Presidio. Luke liked Chinese food, but he'd never been to a banquet. There were about twenty people in a private room at the back of the restaurant on Grant St, all nurses, doctors, and some orderlies. The host doctor kept insisting on new exotic plates of food brought to the tables until everyone was bloated and couldn't consume another bite. The only thing that saved him from serious indigestion was the carbonated apple juice that the waitresses kept supplying.

A week later, Luke found a sales trainee position with Procter and Gamble consumer products division and would start in two-weeks. He celebrated with Jody at their usual place at the bar and she said they didn't need to meet at the bar anymore. He could come by her place in Tiburon. She gave him her address which he could walk to from the Major's apartment complex.

Like Jody, Luke was divorced and had been married for only two years through graduate school. He wasn't experienced with women and perhaps it showed; perhaps that's what Jody saw and liked about him. Several times that summer he went to her place, and they would meet by the pool, and they would drink gin and tonics which she kept bringing out from her ground floor unit. She was a little tipsy on one of those afternoons, and a little strange. She suggested that they go into her apartment. Once inside, she put her arms around him, and he complied. He was attracted to her but not bursting with desire. The last time with a woman had been with his divorced wife.

Jody led him by the hand into her bedroom and undid the top buttons of his shirt and then began undressing herself.

"Well, what are you waiting for?" she said.

He took off his shirt and trousers but left on his underwear. He had an obvious erection which made him feel unexpectedly embarrassed. He noticed several pharmaceutical pill bottles on her bed stand and he asked her what they were for. Was she ill? No, she said, just nervous a lot and not sleeping well. The pills helped.

"They keep me going. You don't want to know what I see every day."

"You gave me some clues when we first met at the bar."

"I think I'm ready for a country clinic, no more army hospital."

She had slipped off her remaining clothes and had lain on the bed.

"Make love to me, Luke, would you?"

What did Luke know about love? He was very aroused now, but he took off his underwear after getting under the sheets. She put a hand on him, and he felt then that he could give her all she could possibly want. He rolled over on her, supporting his weight, slowly penetrating her, rhythmically moving his hips at first but then being overtaken by sensation, he quickened until he became lost in thrusting; then when he thought he might orgasm, Jody suddenly wanted him off her, and she pulled away. He was too aroused to stop easily but she insisted.

"I can't do this, I'm sorry." she said and covered herself.

He apologized, although he wasn't sure why. He had only done what he thought she wanted. He was sorry but he didn't understand. She was such a gentle, sweet woman. That afternoon Jody finished her gin and tonic with a pill from her little plastic bottle on the bed table. She wasn't dismissive toward him, but she was no longer the Jody he had known. That was the last he saw of her.

That weekend he went drinking in Sausalito village with Major Terry who could hold his liquor. It was a relief to Luke to see him in civilian clothing. He became a red-faced Irishman with drink, loquacious and jolly, instead of the tight-lipped, stolid commander. Although they had eaten some snacks at the bar, they were both moderately drunk by the time they left the village and started back to Tiburon. The major was driving slowly, keeping a controlled grip on a careful ride back when they were overtaken and cut off by a speeding Mercedes. *Sonofabitch*, Terry shouted and accelerated up behind the Mercedes, blowing his horn and tailgating.

"Let the fucker go," Luke pleaded.

Luke was afraid they were going to have an accident. But Terry insisted, playing car tag with the Mercedes. When they arrived at the complex and the underground parking, their antagonist followed them and skidded to a stop beside them. Terry let down his driver side window and shouted at the guy.

"What the fuck, man, you trying to cause an accident?"

The driver got out and started toward them. The Major jumped from the car and assumed a defensive stance. The assailant, a solid looking guy, maybe six feet, shot a round-house right hand straight at the major who side stepped, simultaneously grasping the assailant's arm and wrist, moving with the momentum and direction of the blow when he abruptly changed direction and reversed the momentum into a semi-circle, taking the man off balance and down hard onto his back, all in an instant. The Major held fast on the man's wrist in a lock. The assailant had been subdued. As he tried to struggle, the major applied pressure on the locked wrist which caused the man to wince and plead.

"Okay, okay", he cried. The major continued to hold him supine on the parking lot concrete.

"Look, buddy, you dangerously overtook us on the road, driving like a maniac. I was just minding my own business, going slowly but carefully. Let's call it a night and you be on your way, all right? Or I'll break your goddamn wrist right now!" He applied pressure to his hold on the man's wrist twisted in an unnatural position.

"All right, okay, I got it," the man cried. Terry let him up and took a semi-fighting stance, in case the man wanted to go another round. But he brushed himself off and went back to his car and got in without any further conflict and drove off.

Terry seemed quite sober now as they walked to their apartment.

"What do you call that?" Luke asked.

"What?"

"How you fixed that guy."

"An unfortunate circumstance."

"No, the way you did it. Never seen anything like it."

"Aikido."

"What?"

"A kind of Japanese self-defense"

It was amazing and unforgettable. Luke now had new respect and awe for the Major. He was a lot more than just a uniform with decorations.

A week before Luke was to report to Proctor and Gamble, the major threw a party in the apartment on a Friday night. There were a few people from the Presidio, some from the complex and others. Almost all were singles, including an equal share of unattached women. Luke got cozy with one of the women, dancing with her and chatting her up.

"Are you in the military?" he asked. Lina was her name.

"No way, I just tagged along with one of the ladies here."

"What do you do?"

"I own a shop."

"Yeah, well, what kind of shop? Where?"

"You ask a lot of questions."

"Isn't that what we're here for, socializing?"

"Let's dispense with the chat. You want to get laid, don't you?"

Luke was momentarily taken back by her forward question. He'd never encountered anything quite like this before. Her inquiry was not a joke. Lina had a solid athletic physique and an attractive face and complementary long hair. She had put a hand on his shoulder.

"How about you show me your room in this establishment?"

Luke made a quick survey of the room full of dancers, duet conversations and drinkers. The Rolling Stones were blasting from the stereo with *Ruby Tuesday*. The Major had a hand up on the wall, leaning in over a buxom young woman, trying to confine her to his drunken wooing.

Lina followed Luke down the hall into his room and he closed the door behind them, locking it.

"Where's your bed, man?"

He hated that appellation and didn't respond. He rolled out the soft thick Oriental carpet he'd been sleeping on since he moved in, not having had money or means to move in a real bed. He'd get a real bed with sheets and blankets when he got his first check.

He put the light dimmer switch on low and started taking off his clothes. She didn't take off her clothes but unbuttoned her blouse and lifted her dress and took off her under pants. She had a solid body and above average breasts with small protruding nipples. It was as if she was planning and expecting a quickie for other motives beyond pleasure. Luke didn't care after his recent adventure with Jody. Now his need was his first consideration.

As he tried to kiss her, she turned her head away. No kissing, she ordered. *Jesus, what was going on?* he thought.

"Just fuck me. You know how to do that, don't you?" she said.

And so, he did, and they quickly came together loudly. The music outside the room was so loud, no one would have heard them.

It was odd. No post-coital warmth or endearment, nothing. She jumped up, put on her underpants, and straightened her blouse and skirt. She gave him a pleasant warm peck of thanks on the cheek and left the room.

It took him a few minutes to regain his composure and get dressed. When he rejoined the party, he couldn't find her. He asked several women if they knew Lina, and none did. She had slipped out into the night and into the untraceable. Had he been used? Had he been chosen at random to inseminate her? He'd heard about women who did such a thing and planned to raise a child by themselves without the complications of a father, marriage, and the whole sticky mess. In any case, why had he been so careless as to not use something, swept away by being too much in the moment without reflection? Freedom had become an empty loose word.

Summer of Idiocy was a better name for what he saw in the streets that summer. The war across the Pacific in Vietnam raged more than ever, the North Vietnamese and the Viet Cong on a roll, while in San Francisco it seemed everyone was still just talking love, wearing flowers, and smoking dope. It was all bewildering. Where was the meaning in those boys in the Presidio hospital with destroyed bodies? The price of freedom? That notion had to be empty to them now. It was to him. His sexual encounters, first with

Jody and then with Lina, were also empty. The needless incident between the Major and the stranger in the parking lot had left him shaken. It belonged with the same insanity that put all those broken young men in the hospital. When he got back into the city, he'd join the weekend peace marches. But for now, he had to focus his mind elsewhere.

He pondered what new model car P&G was going to supply him with when he started training in his sales job, and then remembering a couple of pretty faces he'd often seen around the apartment complex, he fantasized about meeting them. Tomorrow was Sunday. It was predicted to be warm without the usual Bay overcast. In the afternoon he would make a tall gin and tonic and lie by the pool where tenants would be coming out to lounge, read, drink, and socialize.

The Imaginary Jew

I thought I had found the right Barney Groschinger in Sacramento when I sent him a copy of my recently published book with the inscription EFT. Only three Barney Groschingers came up on Google. The best guess was the one my age, and so I figured it had to be him. The EFT was the exclamatory acronym he coined for *Every Fucking Time*, which expressed for him his ongoing exasperation with his many problems during the years I knew him. There has been no response from him so far.

Fat and homely with a round fleshy face and horn-rimmed glasses, he characterized himself as a Teaneck, New Jersey Jew, which he was not. He often used Yiddish expressions to underscore his assumed pose. In fact, to this day fifty years later, all the Yiddish words I know, I owe to him.

Barney was partly a product of that time in our lives, the 60s, when the stretch from high school through college to adulthood was often less of a straight line than it had been for prior generations. The liberation of the era was a big responsibility which few of us handled with grace, much less with direction.

Barney and I shared a small garage apartment duplex, he on one side and I on the other. I remember him introducing himself when I moved in, a business major at our local university. He suggested we share a glass of wine, but his

Russ Desaulnier

being without, he suggested we walk to the corner liquor store and get to know each other on the way. In route, he wanted me to know that he was a *gansa macher*, a mover and shaker, and whatever it took he was going to make a million before he was thirty. Maybe so, but his wallet was empty that day when it came time to pay for the wine. *Schnorrer.*

On his flip side, Barney was politically progressive and had vehemently supported LBJ for President and Pat Brown against Ronald Reagan for governor of California. When Reagan won, Barney composed a protest ditty on his guitar that roasted the actor. Barney was a *hakham mensch* in disguise.

I sometimes felt Barney was like an allergy, not harmful, but a mild nuisance and irritation. He had a way of showing up at my doorstep at inopportune times. For years he drove the same old Volkswagen which inside looked like a dumpster, a repository of jumbled dirty clothes and lots of trash. It was this kind of behavior that earned him the nickname *The Crow* by one of our mutual acquaintances in Long Beach. Barney appeared oblivious to living in filth, trash, and confusion. *Schmutsik!*

Living next door to him, I sometimes got to see the inside of his apartment which verified his reputation. For a short time, he had a woman living with him, a few years older, who kept the place orderly and clean, but that didn't last. She complained about his dirty habits and his sexual proclivities outside the normal range, as she put it, when she hurriedly escaped the duplex one afternoon when Barney wasn't around, and she was never seen again. He never discussed it except to say the woman was *meshugganer.*

Barney always had itinerant jobs. As a result of one his more interesting jobs, I was once provided with one of the best lunches I'd ever had. For several months he had worked on a fishing boat that supplied the Japanese market with the prized urchin orange-colored roe. It was a lucrative job which Barney, like a human walrus, could handle with ease, diving down as much as thirty feet to scoop up the spiny creatures. A side benefit was his coming back with other items taken from the sea bottom. One day he showed up at my place with two large red abalone, already a threatened species in the 60s. He removed them from their mother of pearl shells, trimmed and sliced the large white meaty foot of each mollusk and fried the slices with butter in my iron skillet. To this day, I have never tasted anything so rare and exotic as that meal, which might only be possible nowadays at a very high-priced Tokyo seafood restaurant.

One of my worst memories of living next door to him was one night around 2 am when a tow truck arrived out back in the alley, attempting to hook and tow away his Volkswagen for repossession. Barney was beside himself but powerless to do anything. The two burly men doing the towing were unmoved by Barney's wailing and begging them to let it wait until he could make a payment first thing in the morning when the banks opened. How could one live and work without a car? It was too late. And that was final. I felt sorry for him, and I taxied him to school that week, to his bank and the car dealership to make up his payments plus late fees and the cost of towing. Barney could only smolder and utter "EFT!"

We had both been to El Camino Junior College before transferring to Long Beach State College and while we were at the JC, we had both taken the ethics course taught by touted Professor Burkhardt to satisfy a humanities credit. It was one of the most illuminating courses I had ever taken.

Upon reflection, I wonder how much influence this class worked on Barney's choices. Doing the right thing seemed like a straight-forward proposition, but if you were often broke or struggling to pay rent and eat, you might be tempted to cut an ethical corner here and there to meet your needs. Barney and I had some intense discussions about the dilemmas of needs-fulfillment in those days.

I remember grocery shopping with Barney down the street at our big Alpha Beta chain store. As he passed the deli case, he'd sometimes covertly pick up a package of sliced ham, salami or other deli meat, peel off the packaging by feel while nonchalantly keeping watch and then form the meat into a tight roll and after one last look to see if the coast was clear, he'd stuff the roll into his mouth like a big seabird swallowing a fish. *Chazer*. I was always surprised he didn't choke. He would do this with whatever other food item presented an easy hand to mouth maneuver as he circulated around the store, putting other items he intended to purchase into the cart. By the time his shopping and grazing was done, he would have had plenty enough to eat until dinner time. I think store surveillance has probably become more effective these days at preventing such petty crimes with sophisticated optics and electronics, although I would guess there are a lot more desperate, hungry souls now than there were in the 60s.

After I graduated from the college, I moved to a bigger place I could afford, having acquired a 9 to 5 job at the Long Beach Press Telegram copy desk, an entry level newspaper position I got because of Preston Gary, the faculty supervisor of the college newspaper on which I had written for several semesters.

Barney and I lost touch. College friendships were generally not any more deeply wrought and lasting than those made in high school. People moved on. At that age, one is full of future hopes with little inclination to look back, especially if you were advancing. Barney wasn't advancing. In the years that followed, he'd show up periodically like a human salmon swimming upstream against the current, looking the worse for wear and still driving the same trash filled Volkswagen. Although I sometimes felt ambivalent about Barney, there was no denying a certain affection between us, established by the many happy times we'd had during those undergrad years at the duplex and reinforced by a stretch of time lacking similar close camaraderie.

My last meeting with Barney came about near the turn of the decade when he called and was surprised that I had kept the same number. He said he was just up from San Diego. He wanted to see me and asked for my address. I gave it to him and told him to come over.

"Barney, my man, how great to see you." I was determined to overcome my wavering sincerity. He'd lost a lot of weight and was deeply tanned.

"It's been a while. Life treating you well?" he asked.

"I can't complain," I said.

"I can! My albacore boat went out of business. Who knows why? The captain was such a *momzer*. It was too late in the season to catch another boat."

"You can't stay away from the sea, can you, Barney?"

I remembered the years I had known him at the duplex that the sea had always called him. His recurring dream was owning a boat, not just any boat but something special which he had illustrated once by taking me down to a Long Beach boat yard to show me someone's unfinished hull of a fifty-foot schooner. The hull was made of cement formed around a steel frame with heavy wire mesh. I didn't know anything about boats or boating, being a land animal, but I saw the charm in the design of the schooner's captain quarters, a smaller version of the back end of the big wooden, cannon-bearing, square-sailed ships often portrayed in period movies. He told me one could make a fine sea-worthy craft economically with cement, which he would do one day. I didn't doubt that he could if he ever could put together enough discretionary money. *Toygevdik mensch.*

He was calmer now, making no attempts at needling or irony, no *gansa macher* putting on.

"You look well," I said.

"I lost forty pounds," he replied. "Work on the boats is hard."

"What are you going to do now?"

"I'm getting unemployment insurance. That should give me time to sort things out. And you?"

I told him about my work at the newspaper, that I wasn't thinking too far ahead. Like him, I was now beyond the 1-A draft classification, having reached the magical age of 28, neither young nor old, we could still be called if Viet Nam heated up enough, but for the moment the draft board was content to call on younger cannon fodder.

"How about a bite? I was about to make a sandwich for lunch when you called. Ham and cheese?"

I whipped up a couple sandwiches, poured out some tea and settled down to hear his story. He'd been party to some big albacore catches on his boat and had banked, instead of blowing it all. That was fresh. He had realized early on after receipt of his BA in business that he didn't fit into a straight job in the corporate world, nor did he especially want one after a six-month trial at Mattel Inc., the giant toy manufacturer in LA. I shared his disillusion with our college education that guaranteed nothing, although we had once believed otherwise. I had merely got lucky, finding a decent job because of a caring faculty advisor.

Barney was still big but not the tub of lard he used to be. And his demeanor was much more subdued and sincere. He didn't say *EFT* at all, not even once for the sake of nostalgia. I poured him more tea and excused myself to the bathroom. When I came back, he was standing, looking out my living room bay window, and drinking his cup of tea.

"Good old Long Beach, huh? We've had some good times here."

"It's like we never cut the umbilical cord with the college," I said

"I have!" Barney countered. "I don't think I'll be here for long."

"Back to San Diego?"

"Nope, I'm going north, the Bay area, Sacramento, I'm not sure yet."

We finished our sandwiches and discussed guys from our old circle of friends—Brewer, Robertson, and Merrill, all scattered around the map. We barely touched on the topic of women. He said he'd briefly been with a *zaftik* Mexican woman in San Diego, but she had too many family strings attached. As for myself, I was still looking.

After that visit I didn't think much about Barney for a week or so until I thought to look for my old gold pocket watch. I always kept it nearby on the secretary in the catchall abalone shell full of assorted odds and ends, keys and coins. The watch had been an accessory in my hippy days, including bell bottoms, at the peak of the 60s. Since then, the watch had become more of just a keepsake. Not finding the watch in the abalone shell, I searched everywhere through

Russ Desaulnier

my old secretary desk compartments and drawers to no avail. Marty was the only one who had been alone in my space long enough to pocket the watch. I felt my adrenaline spike when I envisioned Barney lifting the watch and then posing himself nonchalantly at my bay window. *Gonif!* I felt violated and betrayed for days and foolish for offering my hospitality. It didn't help my anger when I received a card from him a month later, telling me he was happily working on a salmon boat out of the Sacramento River. *Schmuck!*

The incident had drilled deep to my core, and I was still fuming when l became distracted by the good fortune of a date with an attractive young woman from the Press Telegram offices. I had to dress a little for the occasion, which meant slacks, pressed shirt, and a sport coat. I went through several changes, trying to decide how I looked best. I had to laugh at my fuss which I thought more appropriate to a young nervous woman on a first date. I hadn't been out with a fine woman in a long time. Sorting through my wardrobe, I came across my old hound's tooth bell bottoms which had slipped off their hanger and were lying in a crumpled heap in the back of the closet. When I grasped the pants to pick them up, I found a lump in the tiny front pocket at the belt line. Shock and delight! It was my watch! How had I forgotten it? The tiny pocket, I later discovered, was originally designed in the 19th century for pocket watches. Talk about irony! I'd worn the watch with my chic hippy look of bell bottoms, vest, and watch several weeks before for a wild party, and I had arrived home more than little drunk. Just like me to be absent-minded and always looking for something I'd misplaced. My mother, in one of her rare attempts at humor, used to claim I would have misplaced my bum if it hadn't been attached.

I had been dead wrong about Barney, and I felt ashamed of my haste in judging him and stupid about mindlessly misplacing the watch. But that evening I was able to go out on my date, feeling relieved of the *kvetch* I had been carrying around about the watch. I thought ordering the grilled salmon for dinner only appropriate, and my date, wanting to be agreeable, said she'd have the same. I ordered us two glasses of a dry white house wine and I proposed a toast to Barney. Naturally, she was curious and wanted to know who Barney was.

"Well, Barney was a guy I knew in my undergrad days who was an odd sort of character who wasn't Jewish but who acted as if he was, for reasons unknown, maybe because of his growing up in a Jewish neighborhood in Teaneck, New Jersey which he'd often mentioned. There was a time when he was going to become a hotshot businessman, a *gansa macher*, as he put it, a mover and a shaker, but as it turned out he became a fisherman, currently up north, and right now you might be eating Chinook salmon he caught."

I raised my glass and toasted, "To Barney, *mazel tov*."

May in Paris

The most travel Burt Paisley had ever done was his visit to Niagara Falls in his senior year at Kensington High School. Later, he'd been to Rochester and Erie on two separate occasions, but those places didn't count as remarkable. After high school, he continued at technical college and got an associate degree in office management and accounting. That seemed to fit his aptitude for keeping order, which he practiced as a matter of lifestyle. His apartment just off Eggert Road in the suburbs of Buffalo reflected his orderly life, spare and clean. Everything had a place. His one concession to the extraordinary was perhaps his hobby and fascination with collecting and watching old black and white movies.

During the recession of 2008, he lost his office management job at Coastal Mills, which left many things to be considered. Fortunately, his sober attention to finances as well most other things, would stead him well. He had meticulously saved his money. But the loss of an accustomed schedule and the unplanned blank days that lay before him began to work a change in him that he didn't recognize. So many unemployed days brought more focus to his solitary existence accompanied by an intensified sense of emptiness and loneliness.

While visiting his old friend Jim Kern from middle school days who had an office cleaning business, Burt asked his friend what he thought he should do now that he was footloose. Jim would happily connect him if one of his clients needed a manager, but for the moment there was nothing since the recession had slowed everything.

"Burt, you have no responsibilities, and you have some money and time, why not travel a bit? Do you good."

His friend's suggestion loomed over him for days. If that were something he could do, where? You just can't blindly stick your finger on the map and make that a destination. There had to be a reason, a contact, a relative, something. For the first time in years, Burt began to realize how narrow his life had been. He would stop in at the travel office on Bailey Avenue and pick up some brochures on travel packages. Meanwhile, Jim and his wife Alice invited him to dinner.

"If I were you, I'd go to Paris, the city of lights," Alice said over dessert.

"Paris? I don't know anyone there and I don't speak French!" he replied.

"Burt, I have a friend there who might be glad to show you around."

And so, the curtain was drawn back on an intriguing prospect that had never occurred to Burt, Paris? The more Alice talked about her friend Charlotte, the more he became interested. Charlotte had become her close friend in the year she'd spent as an exchange student from France at Bennett High where Alice had gone to school. After Charlotte returned to France, she and Alice had continued their acquaintance, becoming pen pals with an exchange of emails. Charlotte had finished school at the Sorbonne and now worked at a Parisian publishing house. Alice emphasized that her friend was fluent in English, and still single.

Burt chose a modest ten-day package and round trip from New York to Paris, including connecting flights from Buffalo and return. Alice liked him and had apparently made a case for him to Charlotte and his visit to Paris. Charlotte replied she'd be glad to show him around within the limitations of her job responsibilities. Alice showed him her high school picture from seven years ago: a pleasant looking girl with a genuine smile. But this was not a date; it was a friendly arrangement. Burt's record with women was wanting, even though he was a relatively good-looking man of thirty. He found it hard to make conversation with women. At least that had been his limited experience so far with the few girls he'd found in the office staff at Coastal Mills. But perhaps this would be different? The French, after all, were known for their great proclivity for romance. But he didn't want to let himself get foolishly hopeful in that direction, and so he concentrated on his Paris itinerary which had to include the Versailles palace, Napoleon's tomb, the Champs Elyse, Notre Dame cathedral, the Louvre, and of course, a stroll along the left bank of the Seine. As a working woman in the city, Charlotte would know the best places to dine without costing an arm and a leg. He felt swept up in a wave of expectation he'd never felt before.

His tour package had him booked at the modest Les Tournelles Hotel at a reasonable $100 per night. Charlotte's place was not far from his hotel in the Marais district, and she had emailed him a plan to meet in the Place de Vosges, a lovely little park a short walk from the Tournelles hotel. She would be wearing a red beret (what else?), a kerchief around her neck, a white blouse, and a black skirt, over all a flag he could not miss. She could have come to the hotel, he thought, but she must have felt the park meeting more appropriate for starters and to Burt's thinking, their meeting in a park was romantic.

She was indeed easy to spot at the park, on time as agreed. As they walked toward each other, she came into focus. This was not the girl in the high school picture—far from it. She looked more his age, in her thirties, with decidedly Marlene Dietrich looks, notably the fine features and thin plucked eyebrows. In any case, she was a transformation from what he'd expected. Her hair was now blondish whereas it had been brunette in the photo, and a thick lock of hair hung from under her beret, half covering her right eye, like nothing he'd ever seen among the office girls in Buffalo. He squared his shoulders and reflexively ran his fingers through his hair.

"Monsieur Paisley, oui?"

"Yes, and you are Charlotte Mazure."

"I am pleased to meet you, Burt."

"And I you."

"I have had so little opportunity to speak English since I was in Buffalo."

"Alice couldn't say enough nice things about you."

"I am sure she exaggerated." On this last word, he noted her accent.

Alice hadn't any idea how her old high school friend, the exchange student, had grown and changed, he thought. A woman with such looks surprised him with her warmth and relaxed nature. He was not accustomed to the company of someone so attractive, so sophisticated. He asked her to take them to a nearby restaurant where they could have lunch and coffee, a place she might go with a friend on an average day. The Café Hugo was near a corner of the park,

Russ Desaulnier

a *brasserie*, where they each had *le plat de jour*—soup, salad, baguette, and a terrine of pate. They finished with a couple cups of coffee and chatted for two hours.

Burt gave her a description of his past job and how he would look for something new when the recession saw some relief, and Charlotte described her job at the publisher, editing book galleys in English, Spanish, and in French. She was from Toulouse and missed the slower pace of the country, but there was so little opportunity for work, and her friends from her Sorbonne days were in Paris. He felt he had to paint something better than what he usually thought of Buffalo, but there was so little to describe. Charlotte remembered a little about Buffalo from her student exchange year but mainly only Bennett High and her friend Alice. It had been an American steel town and its people and ways had changed little since. But he did describe the ubiquitous beef on weck sandwich that could be found in almost all drinking establishments and the great lakes nearby which had been brought back from their near death in the 70s. Her attentiveness and questions for details encouraged him, so that he then segued to old movies. Did she know *All About Eve* with Betty Davis? Surely, she knew *Casablanca*. She did, of course. Everyone knows that movie. He restrained from dropping the famous line, *we'll always have Paris*.

"Do you know the movie *Les Enfants de Paradise*? The Children of Paradise," Charlotte asked. He didn't, and then she went into a long explication of the movie and how it was one of the greatest films ever made. Even Marlon Brando was known to have chosen it as the greatest. Burt made a mental note to purchase the movie with subtitles when he got back. As she talked about the film, he could see the changing shades of her face as she talked about the female lead, a courtesan, and how she responded to the love from four diverse suitors. At that point in their conversation, Charlotte was fitting the rumored stereotype he had of French women. Were they all in love with love?

He had only been seriously in love once and near asking the girl to marry him, but then he procrastinated until it became too late because she impatiently took up with someone else. The memory didn't seem worth telling Charlotte about. Judy Townsend was never as glamorous or interesting as Charlotte.

Charlotte had to get back to work but asked him to come by her place and pick her up about nine that evening. Her place was close to the Seine. They would have a little wine and walk it off along the river that passed by Notre Dame. She wrote out her address on a card and gave it to him and told him to show the address to a cab driver and he would be dropped off in front of her place in minutes from the Tournelles Hotel.

They stopped in three different bars and drank small glasses of house wine enroute from her building to the Seine River and when they arrived, they walked along the famous left bank. She told him some of the history of Notre Dame as they passed. Construction began in the 12th century and continued through the 13thcentury. She had not seen the black and white movie *The Hunchback of Notre Dame*, starring British actor Charles Laughton, but she had read the novel by Victor Hugo in high school. Burt had never read the novel but knew the movie well. A young Maureen Ohara played the vulnerable gypsy girl Esmeralda.

Charlotte suggested he stop in and see her place before his going back to his hotel. She would make them a snack and some hot chocolate for a night cap. In the lore of black and white movies this was understood as an invitation to be intimate, but that was more than fifty years ago. It would be audacious to presume this modern educated woman was inviting him for intimacy after she'd only met him eleven hours ago. He didn't entertain any such thoughts of that outcome. He was happy to have had the interested attention of such a lovely woman on his first full day in Paris, the storied city he had never thought of seeing until coincidences conspired to land him there.

Charlotte toasted some slices of baguette and spread them with a tangy soft cheese and poured off two mugs of hot chocolate she brewed in a saucepan. She opened the door length window of her fifth-floor tiny apartment and let in a cool evening breeze. He couldn't remember feeling so content.

"I would offer to make love, but I'm indisposed at the moment." Charlotte said, as if she were simply commenting on the cooling of the room with the breeze. "I hope you will understand."

He had to catch his breath and compose his thoughts. He hardly knew how to respond to this unexpected and forward declaration.

"I..ah…um..I had no such expectations."

"That is such a relief. I like you very, very much, Burt.

"Thank you for such a wonderful time today and this evening."

"You are such a gentleman for not asking me to explain."

"That would never occur to me."

"Yes, I know. My intuition told me."

When it came time to leave, she embraced him at her door and gave him a warm kiss, neither sensual nor just platonic. They would see each other in two days. Until then, he should take in the Louvre for some deep and awe-inspiring distraction. He felt so lifted by the evening, he decided to walk back to his hotel. It wasn't far and he was good at reading directions and landmarks. He knew he had to go east for about a mile and once in the right *arrondissement,* as they called it, he would ask someone the whereabouts of the Tournelles if he wasn't finding it.

She was right about the Louvre. It was like entering into another world, another atmosphere, another universe. He became lost and intoxicated in its huge galleries and billboard sized canvases by famous French, Dutch, and Italian painters from centuries past. He had seen a few things at the Buffalo Art Museum, but this was so much more than anything he had known, as was Charlotte.

Over his last nine days in Paris, with a couple days in between when they didn't see each other, Charlotte accompanied him to all those sites he'd wanted to see, culminating in a day's trip out to Versailles. It was easy to see why Louis XIV was the Sun King. The Versailles shone as brightly as did Charlotte, and he thought he might be falling in love with her. On their last evening together, he treated her to a fine dinner at Le Petit Marche, a top billed restaurant in the neighborhood of his hotel. They polished off a smooth 2005 Saint-Emilion cabernet with rack of lamb, potatoes au gratin and spring peas. The bill was no more than one would pay at a good Ellicott St. restaurant in downtown Buffalo, but he suspected the Petit Marche meal was much better. What great pleasure it was to dine and drink with such an elegant, kind woman.

She was so educated and cultivated, he tried not to think of his lacking by comparison. He knew a few words in French but he was too embarrassed to use them with her and certainly he would not confess *je t'aime* to her, which he considered from all angles for days. It was too much, too soon, and she might very well reject him as immature for rushing to something he couldn't possibly know in such a short time. Or she might accuse him of simply being self-deceived, infatuated and dazzled by Paris. When it was time to say goodbye, he had settled on *I will always care for you very much, Charlotte, and I hope to see you again someday.*

And so it was, and Burt Paisley would never be the same again.

Swinging Guys

A lec and I had known each other since the swinging sixties. Alec lived two blocks up on Strathmore from where I lived in the Sigma Nu house on Gayley during my college years at UCLA. After college, I lived a world away from Alec and West LA to the south in Long Beach. Whereas I was heading to an academic life, he was developing a career in the production of Hollywood films. I remember early on when he got his first big job for $500 a week as an assistant production manager on a Western being made near Monterrey, Mexico. I had to admit I was envious. I was near broke all the time, working as a sub teacher and part time clerking in a liquor store, while he was making what was a fortune in those days.

It is strange how we can be so without vision in the moment. We rarely see things as they are, only in retrospect. I often feel I have lived my whole life without ever being much aware in the moment, but maybe if I had been aware, I might never have lived such a variety of lives.

I won't bother you, dear reader, with the early years, except to point out when Alec was coming down to Long Beach for a weekend, he would ask me to fix him up. I usually did this by having a current girlfriend ask along a friend to join us for the weekend of fun, dinners, maybe a show, etc. When I went up to his place, a hilltop house of his

Russ Desaulnier

own construction in Laurel Canyon, he'd have a friend of a girlfriend to entertain me. Why not? There were no digital dating services in those days, only personal introductions. Both of us were handy with the ladies, I guess, but I was always looking for love beyond a casual dalliance. I never fell for one of the Hollywood hookups Alec arranged. And he never got serious with any lady from our Long Beach weekends. That is, I never saw him with the same woman twice. But I wasn't any different. I may have come back to Long Beach with a phone number from one of those weekends but never felt inspired to follow up. In retrospect, I don't think any of those women expected callbacks. That was the mores of the 60s and 70s. By the time I was 39, I was feeling some urgency that I didn't understand. I found myself wanting permanence, a home, a wife. Alec's career, meanwhile, continued unbroken from movie to movie, working as a production manager.

I had moved to Santa Barbara in the mid-70s, and I switched my academic pursuits for real estate sales, and I was doing quite well. My only mistakes during that brief era, just before entering the 80s, was thinking I could once again run the 100-yard sprint in seniors' competitive track meets and take on a younger woman eighteen years my junior.

Determined to sprint again, I stretched my legs for weeks until I could bend and touch my palms to the floor without bending my knees. I had been running for several months but not for speed, mainly jogging to lose weight and quit forever the cursed tobacco, and I ran a few 10-kilometer races to get my wind back. I had become trim and felt I could still run a good hundred. Meanwhile, Brianna fell into my life and my bed without much coaxing or courting. I found that a nubile twenty-one-year-old female body could contribute to an older man's delusions about competing in athletics and attempting to peel back his years. As you might expect, Brianna was sweet but unformed and lacking the kind of finish that a man my age required then and in the longer haul. Remember, I wanted a partner. My first lesson about the folly of getting attached to a much younger woman was her inevitable deception. I had told her if she quit smoking for two weeks. I'd give her two hundred dollars. A foolish offer, but I knew she was hurting for money. I didn't want a woman who smoked when it had taken me so much work to quit. I suppose my ulterior motive was to keep her around by checking for the taste or smell of tobacco. She couldn't quit and she couldn't stay loyal. Santa Barbara was a small town and I found out through the grapevine she'd been seen out several times with the same surfer-type guy, two-timing. I didn't get very upset. Had I been much younger, I might have flipped, but I just doubled down with my training, which also let me down. In a practice session a week before the big meet, I came out of the starting blocks with my old characteristic explosive start from high school days and ripped a ham string. I crumpled down into an agonized heap on the track. The pain and the subsequent healing process were a shocking cognitive experience. Not anymore!

I sold a 16-unit apartment building in a good part of town to a doctor I knew and the commission from that kept me going for several months. Meanwhile I met a new woman at a 1980 New Year's party. With the change of the decade and the coming of the momentous 40th birthday, I was in a state of mind that easily accepted notions of fate and karma when I met Muriel, 28, experienced, witty, and sexy gorgeous. She met me halfway with equal magnetic force.

Alec came up to Santa Barbara a few times and grew to love it. He saw the potential for investment, which I encouraged. It didn't take a genius to know where Santa Barbara real estate was headed, one of the most desirable locations in the nation. After all, location is the primary factor of valuable real estate. I already owned a small one-bedroom duplex I'd bought a year before and watched its value near double. Bigger, more desirable duplexes in the Isla Vista neighborhood of the university would be a sure bet for any shrewd investor. I didn't have to sell Alec. The prices for him, his being a resident of West Hollywood, seemed bargain basement, and so he bought three duplexes, all with 20 percent down. Rent income would cover mortgages, taxes, and insurance. The commissions from the sale bought me a few more months on easy street.

It was Thanksgiving 1981 and I asked Muriel to marry me. We walked the Isla Vista beach in old sneakers that got caked with gloopy oil residue, which was everywhere those days, reportedly from natural leaks in the ocean floor. No wonder there were drilling rigs in the distance between the beach and the Channel Islands. With our engagement settled, Muriel gave up her apartment in central Santa Barbara and moved into my little duplex with me.

I got a call from Alec that he'd like to visit and wondered if I could fix him up with someone. I couldn't but Muriel, now my fiancée, could. She had several girlfriends around town. Probably Stephanie would be the best fit, we decided, a real character, always joking, attractive, near 30, and a sometimes actress in local stage productions. She'd have a natural affinity for Alec's involvement in Hollywood, or *Gollywood*, as Stephanie called it.

It was the beginning of the 80s and at Muriel's suggestion I had installed an all-Redwood hot tub ensemble in my small duplex yard, then a voguish thing to do, including a deck, and fencing for privacy. Our early life together living in that duplex was often baptized in that tub under an avocado tree. There couldn't have been a more romantic spot when there was a full moon and we'd had a few tokes while soaking.

Alec took a waterfront hotel in Santa Barbara but came out to our duplex in Isla Vista for an evening to join us and his arranged double date with Stephanie. She seemed to hit it off with Alec and he with her. He would, of course, because she was voluptuous when seen naked getting into our hot tub and settling into the hot bubbling water with the rest of us who were passing around a pipe full of good weed. Stephanie was indeed an actress and put on a show that night, no doubt for Alec's benefit, about whom she'd been informed by Muriel. Most of her comic material came from her store of Saturday Night Live shows and its stars, such as her wonderful impersonation of Gilda Radner's brash reporter Roseanne Roseannadanna and Laraine Newman's Valley girl.

I barbequed skewers of chicken marinated in white wine, garlic and herbs de Provence. Muriel had made a huge mixed salad and there was plenty of Cabernet and Chardonnay. We all got mildly stoned, but thankfully not drunk. I was happy to have Alec there, a big slice of my history, from Westwood to Long Beach to Tijuana weekends and now Santa Barbara. We beamed at each other. He had brought a mouth-watering German chocolate cake from the German bakery in town to add to the festivities, saying it was to mark mine and Muriel's engagement. When I was barbequing the skewers, the girls left Alec and me alone for a while out on the patio.

"The chocolate cake is a nice touch, Alec, thanks," I said.

"All due respect, man, but do you *have* to get married?" He said this with genuine incomprehension and wonder.

"I'm already forty years old, Alec, what the hell!"

"So am I, but I'm in no hurry."

"Maybe you should be."

"Business is good, plenty of fish in the sea, what's the rush?"

"Remember Edie?"

"No, who?"

"The girl who lived across the hall from me in Long Beach. I set you up with her once years ago when you came down from Hollywood. I was down in Long Beach to visit my folks recently to introduce Muriel and I ran into Edie in the Alpha Beta supermarket."

"I don't remember her, man."

"She looked good, prettier than ever really, still living in the same apartment on 7th where I was, and she asked me to remember her to you."

"Oh yeah? What did she say?"

"Tell him to go fuck himself!"

"Wow, what an angry chick, huh?" Alec shrugged and turned his mouth down at the corners in a dismissive expression.

"She'd never mentioned you after your visit back in the day."

"Did she say anything else?"

"Nope. She just wished me good luck was all and made off pushing her shopping cart."

"She sounds like a *Play Misty for Me* case."

I got the reference, but Edie was no psycho, just a typical sweet working girl, unassuming and private, as she was during the time I had lived across the hall from her in that old two-story apartment building. I was perplexed and paused, looking at Alec, expecting some explanation when Muriel returned to the patio.

She and Stephanie had finished their girl parley and wanted to know when we were going to eat. I asked Muriel to put together the kitchen table and pull out the salad from the fridge. I'd bring in the skewers in a minute or two.

It was a lovely dinner by candlelight, Jobim Bossa Nova playing in the background, Alec and Stephanie cozied up to each other, Alec regaling us with anecdotes from his travels in Europe. When the night was over, Alec was taking Stephanie back to her apartment in Sant Barbara, when I was sure he was taking her back to his hotel. He was such a gentleman opening the door of his silver Mercedes for her. He gave me an *abrazo*, a hug as we parted. We had adopted the Spanish tradition years ago when meeting or saying goodbye.

"We'll check out my properties tomorrow, maybe have brunch before I head back to LA. It was a great dinner. Thanks, both of you," he said.

Muriel and I stood and waved goodbye when he pulled out. I'd been in the Mercedes and his other cars over the years. He was a bit of a cowboy on the road, and it could be harrowing sometimes to sit in the passenger seat.

The next morning, I met him at Sambo's breakfast house down on the beach front road in Santa Barbara. He'd called me earlier and told me Rebecca wouldn't be coming. She just wanted to go back to her place that morning. So, I saw no point in asking Muriel to come along. After a late breakfast, Alec and I convened with the property manager with whom I'd connected him. The manager showed a small cash flow for his properties but said those would soon grow. California real estate was appreciating annually with double digit increases, and rents equally increasing, especially in Santa Barbara.

"Hey, man, if you ever can get away, come on down and visit me. l might even fix you up, if you like, who knows? Right?" Alec said, as I saw him off from the property management office.

When I got back home, Muriel was still cleaning up from the night before, still in her robe and looking glum. I asked her if she was all right.

"I had a call from Stephanie this morning, after you left. She was pretty upset, well, hurt and angry. She even broke into tears a few times over the phone."

"So, what's going on?"

"Alec's a beast. He took Stephanie back to his hotel last night and basically raped her and was rough as hell. Not much of friend, your Alec. "Please don't invite him to our wedding."

Mother

He handed the burial urn with his mother's ashes to the Canadian customs officer along with the certifications from the mortician back home in Eugene, Oregon. He had flown to Montreal where his mother had requested her ashes be buried with his father's and the Toussaint clan. He had waited until summer, the season he best remembered in Montreal, also when the ground would be warmed and softened for easy burial. So, while waiting a few months for summer, he had to see his mother's urn daily staring back at him from the fireplace mantel. He'd felt guilty about hiding it from view. Maybe later he would have a breakdown or a crying jag, but in the weeks following her final moments at 90, he had been numb. Perhaps stored emotion would emerge later.

But he felt clean of guilt. He had given everything he could over the last twenty years to be as good a son as he could. An only child, he remembered mostly the old memories from his childhood but not from recent history. From what he knew of his mother's history, she also had been an only child raised by an aunt and doted upon, growing up, as he did, with all the bewilderment that goes with being the sole child in an adult household. Fortunately, he had a nurturing father, who he remembered complaining he had to raise two children, him, and his mother whom his father married just before her 18th birthday.

His Canadian father had gone to England before the war to make his fortune. But when England went into deep recession after the war, as did his father's tool and die works in Birmingham, he decided to take his child bride and their son back to Montreal where his mother and several brothers and sisters then resided. But Montreal was only a brief stop for his parents in their travels that finally landed them in California in the mid fifties. So, while he grew up in California, his grandmother and many of his remaining uncles and aunts in Montreal eventually passed and were buried at Montreal's Cote-des-Neiges cemetery—then finally his father. He had an appointment with the administrative office to expedite the burial of his mother's ashes in the family plot and have her inscribed on the family stone beneath his father. During his short visit he had been invited to stay with Uncle Robert and Aunt Alma just across the St. Lawrence River from old Montreal and its remnants going back 500 years. He hadn't been in Montreal since the late 1970s when he had visited during a whole summer.

He felt he had one foot stuck in his past life growing up, which he supposed everyone losing a parent must feel when life arrives at this stage. Parents give you birth, and you are left to bury them. You are necessarily left reviewing the part you played. He had brought his mother up to Oregon from LA when his father died, hoping he could help make what remained of her life somehow happy, at least comforted. But he realized after a year of resettlement in Oregon, she wasn't going to be much happier. She was diagnosed with depression but would never stay on the prescribed drugs until old age and a broken hip caught up to her.

Despite the French name Toussaint and the family on his grandfather's side harkening back to the time of Louis

XIV and their settlement along the banks of the Saint Lawrence River, the descendants were all Anglo both in language and sympathies. He was now crossing that same great river on the Cartier bridge enroute to St. Lambert, a leafy suburb of ivied red brick homes and affluent Anglophones. He planned to spend ten days there before flying back to Oregon.

Uncle Bob and Aunt Alma offered him a cozy bedroom on the second floor of their house which had belonged to one of their son's now living on the West Coast. But he asked if he could stay out in the garage apartment by the pool for nostalgia's sake and for the ease of shaping up in the pool during the warm June weather. His not being in the house proper would also make for more privacy for everyone. Of course, he could. He had spent a summer in the garage apartment decades ago. The apartment had been majorly upgraded over the years since he'd last stayed there. It even had its own small bathroom so that you didn't have to cross to the house to use the basement bathroom. An antique armoire with empty drawers and a closet had been installed along with a modern king-sized bed and a small sofa under the bay window that had been there in the 70s. A modern ductless heater/cooler system kept the room temperate, while another wall featured a framed copy of a Kinkade pastoral painting. There was a small antique secretary should a resident need to write some letters. No doubt this was where their married children stayed when they visited. The childhood rooms in the house remained vacated museums of their youth, full of sports paraphernalia, and model airplanes.

He couldn't sleep well the first night; he was tossed and turned by persistent dreams of his mother and the strange deja vu imposed by the converted garage in which he was staying. The past and the present converged. In his dreaming, he saw and heard his mother telling him to be careful driving around Montreal streets—just like her to worry. He dreamed about Jacelyn from next door, welcoming him back, still young as she had been in 1978. Then at one point he was back at Cote-des-Neiges, demanding the urn be given back because his mother was still alive and wanted to be let out to rejoin the world. His anger in making his ignored pleas to the cemetery office awakened him in a sweat. He got up and checked the clock which showed only 3 am. He peeked through the bay window blind at the shimmering translucent blue of the pool. He had spent so many afternoons in the pool back in the 70s, clowning around with Uncle Bob's young sons, Alain and Bobbie Jr., playing chase and capture games to their delighted screams. Now he was an old man and couldn't remember the last time he had gone swimming in a pool. His limbs were still stiff and sore from the long plane ride and his head was still heavy with sleep. He had a drink of water and went back to bed and got comfortable in a half-sitting-up position, and he soon floated off to sleep.

After showering the next morning, he eased into the shallow end of the pool and pushed off into a slow breaststroke. He would have liked to swim with an Australian crawl, but his rotator-cuffs would start acting up with the overhead motion of his arms. He'd learned to swim at an early age at the Hamilton YMCA summer camp on Lake Erie where his parents sent him every summer. How proud he'd felt at ten when he had been secure enough to swim with the older boys out to The Pier, an old abandoned structure two hundred yards from the shore.

After a brief swim and dressing, he went through the rear entrance of the house and into the kitchen where Aunt Alma was making breakfast. Uncle Bob was at the kitchen dining table, having coffee. Aunt Alma wanted to know if he'd like some pancakes and bacon, while Uncle Bob poured him some coffee from the table thermos.

"Sleep well?"

"Too many dreams."

"Grief takes a while to get over," Uncle Bob said. "Wasn't too many years ago I buried your dad out there at Cote-des-Neiges. I think about your dad and the others almost every day."

He remembered how he'd got back to California as quick as he could from Japan ten days after his father had died. His mother was a basket case, and his father's ashes were already in Montreal at Cote-des-Neiges. *Time and tide.*

"Do Bobby Jr. and Alain often visit?"

"Not often, but when they can," Uncle Bob said.

He remembered how he had done the best he could to get back from Japan. He'd visit during the Christmas holidays, and in the summer. Always there was an air of formality with his parents as if they were using it to restrain brewing emotions and questions. Having an only child is as difficult for parents as it is for the child, so much expectation all around.

"What happened to Jacelyn next door?"

"When her mom passed on about 20 years ago, she sold the house and moved to Toronto with her husband," Alma said, placing a breakfast plate in front of him."

He had lost track of time. Jacelyn was always young and pretty in his memories, tapping the door of the garage apartment, announcing her arrival on those late summer nights. Sometimes they would swim without splashing and talk in a whisper after they had made love. She would steal back to her house next door as quietly as she had come. It was a summer about which pop songs are sung on AM radio.

When he was a boy at YMCA summer camp on Lake Erie, his mother and father would visit him on some weekends as it was a short drive from Buffalo. They would stay the afternoon and he would cry when it came time for them to leave. Feeling abandoned, he'd watch their green 1950 Ford disappear down the dusty country road. In those early camp years, he always tried to please his father with how well he was learning to throw a baseball. Then they would go down to the beach and eat a picnic lunch his mother had packed for the visit. When he pointed out *The Pier* and told them how he had been able to swim out to it, his mother was alarmed and didn't stop mentioning it until they left in the late afternoon, her last words being that he shouldn't eat before attempting that swim to the pier, and he should be near some bigger boys just in case. Could he wear a floatation device to make the swim? She looked to his father and questioned what kind of people were running the camp that would allow the boys to undertake such risky endeavors. When he was in Japan, a man in his 40s, she would carry on about his being careful driving Japanese roads. She had heard somewhere that the Japanese were crazy drivers like they were pilots in World War II. When he sent a photo of himself and a Japanese girlfriend posed in front of the giant bronze Buddha of Kamakura, she made a fuss in her return letter about not wanting grandchildren who were half Japanese. When he got older, his father's response to most things were that he was merely putting in time, and he acted as if he were disinteresting in most everything except a good meal.

"More coffee, Jim?"

He nodded to his Aunt Alma. Uncle Robert was working on a piece of toast and the morning paper. Jim reflected that the older we get the more we get settled into routine. He knew this about himself—to bed at ten, up at six, water the garden, empty the dish washer, answer correspondences, get dressed, make breakfast, read the paper, all clockwork.

"No lady in your life these days?" Aunt Alma asked while she poured his coffee.

"Nope. Getting used to being on my own."

"I was sorry about that. I rather liked Elaine."

Divorce came like death. You usually didn't expect it, he thought. One day, one or the other decides the world is wider and more inviting than the confines of marriage. In his and Elaine's case, that view infected them both after fifteen years. Neither manufactured any grievance against the other. It was just over. His mother never liked Elaine. He suspected that was just because his mother didn't feel that she had exclusive ownership of his attention anymore while he was married to Elaine. Only children are subject to all kinds of proprietorial attitudes from parents. It comes with the territory.

He excused himself from the breakfast table after the exchange of more talk about family and a general rundown of events over recent years in Montreal. Already the temperature had climbed into the eighties, so he took another dip in the pool, thinking he would try to swim to *The Pier*, enough laps to equal those triumphant 200 yards of his boyhood on Lake Erie.

His mother's high point in life, he thought, was her bowling league while he was still in high school. She bowled with three other women her age at Jola Bowl on Manchester Blvd where she convened every week in competitive matches. She had even won some trophies, one of which he had saved as a memento, an eight-inch chrome skirted woman atop a walnut pedestal about to unleash a bowling ball, awarded for making 200 points in a single game. It was the only time she really had a life in the outside world. He couldn't put an exact time on it, but she retreated from the world when he graduated from college. Perhaps her hysterectomy during that period marked the beginning.

Depression, the disease, hadn't been recognized or treated until the 1970s, and extremes of behavior were simply assigned to quirks of personality or indeterminate sadness. His mother could be pleasant on occasion, but she was mostly sullen and irritable. In the twenty years after his father passed, she was prescribed anti-depressant drugs, but she'd never stay on them, insisting she wasn't unhappy and didn't need them. No one could convince her otherwise.

When he was still at home during high school and his first two years of college, his mother was happier, serving the needs of the two men in her life. He'd never forgot her morning call—*time to rise and shine, sunny Jim!* Upon reflection, her cooking was often plain and tasteless, but what do we know when we're growing up? We have nothing or little to compare. Remembering his early years at home brought back recognition of her warmth and nurturing.

"You know, Jim, your mother was a simple woman but good hearted. She took good care of my older brother, your dad, for fifty years. That's something."

Uncle Robert had paused before the evening dinner to make a toast to Jim's mother, ending with "May God receive her into his kingdom. Amen."

Jim thought back on the first week of her recovery from the hip surgery when he had to help her get down some soft food by spooning it to her.

"Funny, son, this is how it ends. I spoon fed you as a baby and now…"

He didn't know if his mother was being brave or just in the grace of her mild dementia that gave her moments of forgetfulness and sometimes flights of hopefulness. But she was practical and frugal, as she had always been, requesting an inexpensive cremation rather than a costly traditional burial and all that empty ceremony. He couldn't have stood that. In her final week in the rehab center when she struggled to come back from the hip surgery, he sat on her bed, and they watched the television suspended at the foot of the bed. It was a Sunday special playing the Academy best picture of 1989, *Driving Miss Daisy* with Jessica Tandy as Daisy and Morgan Freeman playing the patient, kindly chauffeur. Tandy, who was playing her swan song in that movie, was a crotchety, stubborn old lady who finally came around to loving appreciation of her long-serving, imperturbable chauffeur. As the film wound down to its conclusion, his mother was undeniably moved, and she wore a tearful smile.

While the movie credits rolled, he stepped away to visit the restroom. When he returned, the television had been turned off and his mother lay motionless, eyes closed, a peaceful expression on her face. The attending nurse tried but couldn't find a pulse, to which she responded with a deep sigh. Carefully pulling the bed sheet up over his mother's head, the nurse then turned to him with a face flush with sorrow.

The day before leaving Montreal, he laid a small bouquet of lavender blossoms, his mother's favorite, in front of the Toussaint gravestone, and he scrolled down through the names from grandmother to the uncles and aunts to his father and then lastly to the freshly engraved *Emma Tous-*

saint, 1925-2015, beloved wife of Liam Toussaint.

The mother he loved had departed decades ago, and he had mourned that loss just as long, so now there were no tears left to shed.

The Deal

"Deal?" was his first word when I opened my door. I hadn't seen Kevin Dobbs in six years since I'd moved from Long Beach. The sudden and unexpected appearance of his large penetrating eyes at my door brought such a rush of memories that I felt momentarily light-headed and all I could do was gawk.

"Cool place, Jimmy, you really scored," he said. I could see the nose of his old classic Porsche in the driveway. His hair was much longer, almost to his shoulders, and he had grown a beard. His eyes were as raffish and hypnotic as ever.

"So, what brings you up here?" My voice wavered. I stood at the threshold, not offering him entrance. I felt as frozen as I did on the night out in the Arizona desert on route 66 when I had been awakened from my nap in the back seat by a state policeman's flashlight blasting my sleeping eyes, as he ordered me to show my license. A taillight wasn't working. Kevin calmly explained we were contracted by an LA agency, and we were driving night and day to get the car to its owner in Philadelphia. Upon request, Kevin proffered the registration, our contract, and his license to the officer. It had been an effort to maintain normal breathing while my heart raced. I had already envisioned the officer opening the trunk and going through our suitcases, one loaded with fifty pounds of premium weed sorted into baggies we

Russ Desaulnier

were going to sell through pre-arranged contacts in Philly. But the officer just warned us to get the taillight seen to at the first opportunity. Stupid is all I could think now, while wanting to close the door in Kevin's face or bring this unexpected visit to a quick close and send him on his way. Instead, I let him in.

"Just needed a change, bro. How's life up here?" he asked.

"Good. Would you like a cup of coffee?" I had made some earlier. *Why am I offering him coffee?* Old habits die hard.

"Sure, man, got any sugar?"

We sat at my kitchen table and began to exchange current basics. He'd sold the desert cabin, flipped a few second-hand cars, ran two paper routes for the Long Beach Press Telegram, turned a few (unspecified) deals and was now suffering LA core burnout.

"Do you mind." He had taken out a silver cigarette case full of hand rolled cigarettes. He picked out a joint. "To toast the old days, yeah?"

"I'd prefer you didn't fire it up. I've quit all smoking. Weed too."

"Weed too?" He seemed genuinely surprised. I put a cup of microwaved coffee in front of him and the dish of sugar cubes. I couldn't help myself; I had grown up with the custom of hospitality. He stirred in a third, then a fourth cube of sugar.

"Nice place you have here," he said as he sauntered into my living room. It didn't seem too presumptuous of him. The large bay window looking out onto the Pacific from my Summerland hill was magnetic and I didn't mind sharing, and I did have a fair amount of collected art on my walls, not pricey but all a reflection of my aesthetic. Art had always been something we shared in the Long Beach days from pop and jazz to French movies and novels, all of it now vaguely shrouded in the memory of smoke, both tobacco and marijuana. In Santa Barbara I had cleaned up and starting jogging 10Ks on weekends. I had become lean and clear headed. Dobbs had stayed in his hip mode and grown more in that direction like his hair which he called his "freak flag."

"Hey, man, I like your Lempicka poster," he said, having made a circle and perusal of the living room. "I was in Paris last year and saw a show of her stuff."

He had always been a Francophile and had substituted for high school French classes all over the Long Beach district. He stopped by the kitchen table and plopped two more sugar cubes into his coffee. "Let's step out into your garden and I can have a smoke, all right?"

I agreed of course. I felt a small relief in just getting him out of the house. Perhaps I could bring this unexpected visit to a close while out in the garden. He fired up a cigarette while I kept my distance, but I soon realized he was still smoking Gitanes, the classic black tobacco French cigarette he had always smoked which had given his apartment a distinctive odor during those grad days when we had hung out together.

"So, what's the deal these days?"

I told him a bit about how I had gotten into real estate and what was going on with me. *Deal* was his signature interrogatory expression. There was an element of impertinence in his constant use of the word. I remember he also had a habit of referring to others and their "reality." Bobby reality this or Joey reality that carried an undertone of mockery or scoffing, as if he were above the foibles of others. He was now walking around the garden smoking his Gitane cigarette, sizing, surveying, occasionally just looking over at me with a slight covert smile. He hadn't revealed much in the few minutes we were out in the garden, just that he needed a change.

"Jimmy, you mind if I use your toilet? The coffee, call of nature." I gave him directions down my dark hallway, and I stayed in the garden.

We had first met in the teacher's lounge for lunch break at Lakewood high school in the mid-sixties where we were both on long term substitute assignments, he in French classes and I in senior English. I realized when I sat down across from him that he was studying me and sizing me up. He nodded at me with a sly grin and pushed his rolled-up baggie from his sandwich across the table toward me. It was a time when many of us were hip to the expression *dime bag,* meaning a ten-dollar ounce of marijuana, in those days usually mild weed that could be smoked down to a butt, a *roach*, which got you high but still functional without debilitating effects. I found out he lived just four blocks from me, also in a garage apartment on 1st Street. Soon after we had become acquainted, I discovered we shared an enthusiasm for the French Wave movies then in vogue and the music of the British pop invasion.

I first went by his place on invitation with a girlfriend at the time, but thereafter I would just see him by myself at his place or at school. My girlfriend Barb didn't like him. She allowed that I liked to smoke a little grass now and then, but she herself didn't indulge and she didn't much like Kevin's type and his counter-culture ideas about most everything. At the time, I was still in transition from my working middle-class background from which I had come. Up until the mid-sixties, most of my choices were dictated by those values.

Becoming pals with Kevin was not unwelcome because he came along at a time when I was increasingly questioning everything which up to that point had seemed predictable. I was on track for a fulltime teaching contract at one of the many school districts in the greater LA area upon finishing my MA.

Garage apartments near the college were plentiful in Long Beach, usually a one-bedroom apartment built above a garage, which many of us students rented in those days. They were cheap and fit our spare student lifestyle. Being poor, we often furnished these garrets with a single-size bed that doubled as a couch, and a used dining table would be purchased from the Salvation Army store. Desk, books and shelving were served by a hollow core door set up on wood crates. We ate a cheap diet with a lot of spaghetti, tuna sandwiches or peanut butter and jelly. Most of us kept around a two-dollar gallon jug of Red Mountain or Gallo table wine, while a dime bag of weed would last a month—for me anyway.

Kevin had nicknamed his girlfriend Susan, Zorba, because, he explained, she possessed the *joie de vivre* of that cinematic character. She wore 501 Levis all the time, which I found out were Kevin's preference for his women, as well as for himself. From the first time I went to his apartment, I felt he was holding court, because I was not the only guest, being among several other grad students. There were a lot of meaningless circular discussions around Marshall McLuhan, Sartre, Camus, Kafka and the Beatles. Kevin lounged on his single bed cum-living room couch covered with a Mexican blanket, and an arm draped over Susan's shoulder as if establishing ownership, while they both puffed on Gitanes cigarettes. Donavan, *de jour*, was playing on his Altec Lansing stereo system a tad loud as though he wanted everyone to not lose recognition of his expensive state-of-the-art system and his taste in music.

At the time I did envy his library of music, his sound system, and his silver 1953 classic Porsche. The car was a mystery. All he would say is "I got it." It had to be a windfall that he didn't want anyone to know about. I think he wanted to propagate a personal mystique around himself. He expressed contempt for women who wore heavy makeup and styled hair, all common in the 60s. Magazines and movies of the time featured women with heavy makeup. We need only to remember the likes of Brigitte Bardot, Claudia Cardinale, and the go-go girls. But for Kevin this was all *plastique,* women not worthy of serious consideration, another facet of his personal canon of taste and style.

I hadn't discovered jazz until I made visits to Kevin's place. He had a collection of LPs featuring jazz greats such as Stan Getz, Miles Davis, Thelonious Monk, and others. I acquired the taste. As for the pot, he always had good stuff and I could count on a few tokes whenever I visited. I didn't realize at the time that he constituted a slippery slope into the taste and habit for cannabis.

It wasn't all one way. In retrospect, he was a friend and a stepping-stone. After all, we usually retain some legacy from every significant friend along the way. When sub teaching had become thin, he got me in the door driving for Long Beach's Red Cab part-time which lasted for almost a year. In the same period, he introduced me to the wonders of the 35 mm single reflex camera. Like Kevin, I had also seen Antonioni's *Blow-up* and had the vision of being a slick urban photographer who could use his photography to get women, an ancillary story here in itself. But then in the mid-70s, we both left LA for separate horizons, he to the California high desert surrounding Victorville and I north to Santa Barbara for a fresh start.

"Deal on the room in the back?" he said upon return from the toilet.

"You mean the hole in the side of the hill?" It was a dark, damp cold room, cut into the back of the hill below the landlord's canter-levered main house above. I used the windowless back room exclusively for storage. I knew where Kevin was going with his observation of that space.

He had taken off his camera slung over his shoulder and set it on the kitchen table. I remembered running around Long Beach, shooting almost everything with my Canon. Within two months I was learning the magic of film development and making prints in an improvised dark room in a big closet. More history.

"So, are you going to look for work?" I inquired.

"I got to find a place to live first."

I kept silent, picking up what was left of my breakfast dishes off the kitchen table and carrying them to the sink. I grabbed that morning's News-Press on the counter and slapped it on the table in front of him.

"Here, check the classified."

We chatted a little more before he left with his typical glibness, just saying "later." I watched him as he walked to his Porsche, the tassels on his ankle high custom moccasins swinging with his gait, the collar on his lightweight leather jacket slightly turned up around the neck like Elvis. He revved the Porsche in a parting salute and then was gone. A hot car was the ultimate American male status symbol, closely aligned with having a beautiful woman on one's arm. This was one of the few times I had seen Dobbs without a woman on his arm. My staid Chrysler Cordoba was a necessary part of my job working in real estate. Transporting a client to a listing in a clunker just wasn't done. A two-seater sports car just wouldn't work. As for personal attire, wearing a tie wasn't necessary, but a sharp sport coat with slacks was minimum like a newer comfortable car, implying a degree of an agent's success and his respect for the largest investment most clients would ever make.

Being on the short side, I often had women who were taller than I, especially when they wore heels. This never bothered me and was of no concern to Elaine, my current lady. I think she liked the fact that her height and slim appearance were augmented by the contrast of me at her side. She liked to dress up and step out for date nights. What woman doesn't want to look her best? I always tried to look good for her and invested in some stylish clothes. In one's mid-thirties, a man in his prime can clean up well. I spent more on grooming in those days than at any other time in my life.

The next time I saw Dobbs was at Joe's Café, the most popular greasy spoon in Sant Barbara because of Paco the bartender who was legend for making the strongest drinks around. Happy hours were always a rave. Joe's Café would occasionally be patronized by movie celebrities from Montecito, a tony district just south of the city. A hip crowd also gathered in, including the often-seen Dave Crosby of the then popular CSN band, and the inimitable Joe Cocker. With the booze flowing freely, Joe's got busy around 9 pm. Elaine liked a weekend stiff drink or two as did I, especially since I'd quit smoking. We'd managed to get a couple of stools down at the end of the bar. I was having my usual OJ and Myers rum and Elaine a Margarita. Then at our backs, I heard the familiar "Deal?" It was him.

Of course, I had to introduce Kevin to Elaine. He turned his raffish eyes on her like search lights.

"Pleased to meet you, Mademoiselle" he said, offering a hand. "Wow, you really remind me of Jeanne Moreau."

"How about that," Elaine replied with faux charm. "And you, Monsieur, remind me of nobody." She continued smiling toward Dobbs. "Welcome to Santa Barbara." She could act when she wanted. An uncomfortable silence between the three of us followed. I'd never thought of Elaine resembling the French actress Jeanne Moreau, but it was just like Dobbs to open an introduction with a French culture item to get attention. Sometimes it backfired. We all broke the lull with trying to get another round of drinks at the busy bar. Meanwhile Elaine went back to her Margarita, peering over the wide rim of her glass and flashed me a raised eyebrow. Kevin ordered a Stella Artois beer.

"Guess what? I got a room for a month at the Breakers," he announced. The Breakers motel was on the 101 just south of Santa Barbara. It was an old 1940s landmark that Century 21's broker Walter Deaver had bought and updated. I'd heard in real estate circles that the old motel had been Deaver's trysting spot over the years.

"Well, that ought to make for a nice little holiday on the coast," Elaine piped in. I couldn't tell if Elaine was trying to be ironic or genuinely trying to be nice.

"Jim tells me you are quite a good photographer." She continued. "I think you'll find lots to shoot up here."

With a small stroke to his ego, Dobbs seemed to relax.

Then Elaine proposed a toast to his enjoyment of Santa Barbara. She had learned how to handle all sorts of people as a bank loan officer. The drinks made everything warmer all around. We chatted and drank for another hour. Kevin talked about a photo-cum framing business he'd like to start up if he could find the right living arrangement. Since I'd known him, he always flew by the seat of his pants. He was one of those people who just couldn't work for anyone else, couldn't work in a steady structured situation with rules and fixed schedules. In that way he was an embodiment of the faux freedom that filled the narrative of our generation in the 60s. I had tired of that freedom and had come to agree with Janice Joplin's Bobby McGee song wherein she sang, *freedom's just another word for nothing left to lose.*

We ended the evening with Joe's house special beef dip sandwiches all around. It was pushing 11pm when we all agreed to call it a night and I put the correct amount of money for my tab and Elaine's on the table.

Back in the day, Dobbs often had sold pot whose efficacy was questionable and bought and sold used cars with questionable mechanical reliability. Around 1970 I wanted a new image with a sports car. Dobbs sold me an orange '62 Alpha Romeo Spider which I drove for two weeks until I found I couldn't shift the gears without producing a sickening sound of mashing metal teeth. A repair shop told me the transmission was shot but could be replaced for $250, half what I had paid for the car. For a week or so, I argued with Dobbs to take the car back and refund me to no avail. Yes, it was working fine when I got it. Perhaps, he didn't know it was on the verge. Yes, perhaps I had forced the gear shifting synchro-mesh a little in the weeks I had it. Discussing this mechanical and moral dilemma, our tempers rose but neither of us crossed the line. So finally, I just resold the car to a young transmission mechanic who would replace what it needed at cost, and he gave me $250 for the car which I turned around and put down on a convertible Triumph Mark 3 Spitfire in cream puff condition whose only problem was a worn convertible top. Where and how Dobbs got his classic '53 Porsche remained a secret. There had to be something either not flattering or perhaps something outside the law which he didn't want to reveal.

During the month of Dobbs' residence at the Breakers, I saw him only a few times. When I did see him, he was wearing the same lightweight tan leather jacket. It seemed that he only changed his t shirts and 501 jeans, but his appearance never changed. He met me one late morning for a breakfast on lower State Street at Esau's. The one interesting aspect of these meetings during his days in Santa Barbara was the absence of a clingy young woman at his side. We were drinking continuous cups of coffee in a booth, and he was smoking a Gitane. One could still smoke in restaurants in those days. We had covered Reagan and the coming election, and we had critically parsed *Ordinary People*, a dramatic new movie directed by Robert Redford with Mary Tyler Moore and Donald Sutherland.

"Ordinary people, my eye, they lived in a mansion, had money and everything, nothing ordinary about them," Dobbs was saying.

"I guess none of it matters when you lose a child," I countered, referring to the hook on which the story was hung. Then there was a long pause between us.

"Deal on Elaine? How serious are you?" he asked.

"What's it to you?"

"Just wondering. She's *tres attirante et dramatique*."

"Meaning?"

"Attractive… TTD…. Tall, thin and dramatic. That's your thing, right? Total James reality, eh?"

"What about Dobbs reality? It doesn't seem to be panning out—like a place to live, and a job?"

"Yeah, yeah, yeah, I'm looking. But the job market is worse here than back in Long Beach. Hell, I'm not washing or busing dishes for minimum. That's Mexican reality. I got a small grub stake for something that works. Just got to find the right place."

I wished him luck, stood from the breakfast booth, and dropped some cash on the table to cover the coffee and pie tab and excused myself. I did have to go into my office periodically to check listings and see what calls I might have had on my sole listing of a house on the Mesa, a middle-class neighborhood of mid-priced three-bedroom stucco. I was walking a thread in this new life. But I had to make it work. Even so, I loved my past in LA. I was like that with some memories, sentimental, but in some ways those years in Long Beach didn't seem real, like college itself, a dream you had to let go of and move yourself ahead. I knew of some old grad students who never left the college town, living on the periphery, working peripheral jobs and hanging out at the old watering holes and bistros.

Dobbs was fond of pointing at others for their "bourgeois delights" but when I pointed out that owning a Porsche was just about as bourgeois as one could get, he insisted the car was the product of German genius, reliable and the *sine qua non* of driving, far above anything bourgeois like a Cadillac. He saw himself as an arbiter of hip taste. Where women were concerned, he bragged that he was a "tamer." I had to admit he'd had an impressive string of women.

It was late March and it was his 40th birthday. I decided to drive down to the Breakers and take him out for a brunch. I had run a 10K over the weekend and I had slept like a baby. I felt renewed and open to everything, even feeling some genuine affection for him. *(Or was it affection for the past?)* After all, he was one of the picaresque characters in my life's story. It was a bit of a drive down the coast, no service station, no convenience stores, nothing, just the road separated a few yards from the sand and surf. At the Breakers, the tide churned up on the stacks of rocks piled as a barrier, while gulls dived and screamed. I had a bounce in my step when I knocked on the door of his unit.

"Who is it?" his graveled voice came from within.

"It's me, James."

A minute later he opened the door. He looked terrible, disheveled in a dirty ragged old shirt and pajama bottoms, his hair tangled, his bug eyes red and unfocused.

"Happy b..... Holy shit! what's with you, man. You look awful."

"I'm a lot better now. Believe me. I partied hard this weekend. I shouldn't have taken the black beauties. Man, I haven't slept since I don't know when."

I knew what those were. I had experimented with them in grad school, trying to cram. Powerful black capsules of amphetamine.

"But, man, I'll get some sleep now. I popped a red."

I took a deep breath and tried not to show my disgust. For the first time ever, I felt doom was stalking him. Like the room, he was disheveled. Dirty clothes and candy wrappers were strewn on the floor, and the ash tray next to the bed was full of Gitanes butts. I washed up a glass in the tiny kitchenette and poured him a fresh glass of water and told him to drink it. I knew about reds, otherwise known as Seconal, a barbiturate, that would soon put Dobbs down.

"Yeah, man, my birthday....we..we're, you know, old buddy, we're...Geez....getting fuckin' old."

He was futilely poking around in the debris on the side-board, looking for cigarettes. He found an empty package, screwed it up and tossed it in frustration. "Hey, man, you gotta… ah shit, I forgot, you quit."

His eyes were looking right at me but didn't focus, didn't see, and then his eyeballs rolled upward into his head, and he crumpled to the floor into a heap. He was as limp and heavy as a stack of wet blankets but thankfully still alive when I wrestled him onto the bed and got a pillow under his head. Then I covered him as best I could, cleaned up the sideboard where I placed another fresh glass of water, his wallet and car keys. I swept the floor mess into a pile, turned off the lights and made sure the shades were tightly shut, took his phone off the hook and set the door handle to self-lock and let myself out. He needed to sleep it off.

On the way back up the coast, I fell into thinking about events from our past. One that often came to mind, because it was so painful, was our one token nod to sports with a turn at the YMCA squash courts in Long Beach. He was surprisingly adept at the game. I only kept up with him because of my speed but he had the upper hand with a skill-ful racket. After a half hour of this, the day was brought to an abrupt end when I made a lunge for a low return he was trying to sneak by me, and I popped a ham string. That is what happens to weekend warriors and out of shape once-upon-a-time athletes. The pain was intense. With an arm slung over Dobb's shoulder he got me back to my car. We'd come in my car and so I gave him my keys and he drove me home. Once home, he set me up with a cold pack he assembled from my freezer ice trays. It took a couple weeks to get the leg back to some measure of normalcy. After that I never played a racket sport again.

I had two sales that March and Kevin left the Breakers. He called me and told me he was heading for Ventura. He'd stay in touch, he said. But he didn't. I completed another year in the real estate business, and then the 80s recession began in earnest. Elaine and I were still together, and we decided to get married and make a fresh start in Seattle where there were opportunities for both of us, even some teaching jobs.

All our lives, I guessed, took their predetermined course. Elaine worked until she was six months pregnant, and I had signed in with a fulltime position at an outlying school district to where I had to commute an hour from the city. We'd move out to the suburbs when we could put a down payment together on a house and when my teaching position was secure. There never was an opening at a school district in Southern California when I was looking, but districts around suburban Seattle were hiring and my LA background and my having been out in the world as well as in the classroom was of interest to them. When I interviewed with the asst. district superintendent, he asked me what novel I'd choose for a senior English class, and I shot back confidently without pause, *Madame Bovary*, which made my interviewer smile with satisfaction. Then he wanted to know what American novel I'd choose. That would have to be *Huckleberry Finn*, I replied. I don't know if my answers were the clincher, but I like to think so.

Twenty years flew by, as years do when one has children. Elaine and I had a girl and a boy and finally acquired the three-bedroom house within a fifteen-minute walk of the high school where I worked. So, when the weather was nice, I just left the car at home. I did in fact use *Madame Bovary* a few times for reading assignments and of course

I used *Huckleberry Finn*. Even Hemingway had said it was the greatest American novel, although I found it was a stretch for kids in the new millennia with computers and a much-changed world to accept that a kid going down the Mississippi on a raft had such lofty relevance.

I hadn't thought much about Dobbs over the next twenty years. So much else intervenes in our lives which takes up the room in our consciousness and our daydreams. Some memories get pushed to some obscure corner of the mind, even more so the things we are not proud of and the people we cared the least for. Sometimes I wondered if I really lived through the 60s and 70s because there seemed so little I could account for beyond the high points, like those that appeared on my curriculum vitae that led me directly to where I am now in Seattle. I remembered teaching as a long-term substitute in Lakewood, California. I was a young hotshot with a freshly minted MA and teaching certificate who thought the kids would love me if I made the classes relevant. I just wanted to get them to read. But I would never again try assigning something like *Valley of the Dolls*, a trashy novel, and a good way to open oneself to serious parental complaints or even firing. It was a wonder I only got reprimanded by the department head. That was the same year, 1966, that I met Kevin in the teacher's lounge with his rolled-up plastic baggie.

I am googling Kevin Dobbs, Ventura, California, where he was headed when I last saw him. The first story to come up at the top of the page is about him. It includes a mug shot. His hair is thin, stringy and pure white, his face desiccated and haggard. Only the large penetrating eyes have remained the same.

Man, 60, Arrested in Killing of Other Man Struck in the Head with Hammer:
Ventura Police
LOCAL NEWS
by: Miriam Palmer
Posted: Jun 13, 2000 / 02:18 PM
PDT / Updated: Jun 13, 2000 / 02:19 PM PDT

A 60-year-old man was arrested on suspicion of homicide in the death of a man who was struck in the head with a hammer, Ventura police said Monday. Officers were called to the 300 block of South San Clemente Street about 9:30 p.m. Sunday for a report of a fight in an alleyway, according to a news release from the Ventura Police Department. When they got there, they were directed to a residence near the alleyway and spotted a man leaving. The man, Kevin Dobbs, 60, was detained while officers went inside, where they found a 30-year-old man with a head injury from being struck with a hammer. The victim, who was not identified, was taken to a hospital, where he was pronounced dead. Dobbs was booked on suspicion of homicide. He is being held on $510,000 bail and is due in court Tuesday, according to county inmate records.

Kevin was a lot of things, but he wasn't violent. I was sure he'd simply been defending himself against someone younger and stronger and the deadly blow with a hammer had not been intended as he defended himself against an assault. Not having funds, he hadn't been bailed and probably was being poorly defended by a public defender. I sent an email to him to the address I found for Ventura County jail inmates, wishing him good luck in the trial, hoping he would be exonerated with a plea of self-defense and be given a light sentence, if any. I knew he didn't kill anyone with intent and malice. I never heard back from him.

Two months later, I was able to get the results of his trial in which he pleaded voluntary manslaughter in self-defense and was sentenced to 15 years in the California State penitentiary.

Nippon News

Japan was the most beautiful of experiences and often the most frustrating. But it gave Harry Banks the best paying job he'd ever had at six figures a year. He felt it was a sort of payback for all the penniless checkered years he'd spent in California after graduate school. Teaching school had been his original goal but by the 70s, it seemed that all the good fulltime teaching jobs had been filled by an over-abundance of graduate academics. He had only some short-lived, part-time teaching jobs and then a string of fringe jobs that kept food on the table until the beginning of the 80s landed him in Japan.

AUIS, Aichi University of International Studies, was new and still filling its faculty ranks in the English department when Hiro Yoshihara tapped him for a possible position. Harry had already put in a year around the prefecture teaching conversational English at company classes for Toshiba, Mitsubishi, Honda, Toyota and others when he met Yoshihara in Mie's neighborhood sake bar, or *aka-chochin*, as they are known for the red globular lantern that hung at the entrance.

When Harry arrived in Japan there wasn't a lot of Caucasian foreigners, especially in Nagoya, so he attracted attention. He was a *gaijin*, a foreigner, a description of his person that had ramifications he'd learn with time. Yoshihara approached him in the small bar and offered him a drink, not so unusual, when many sought the opportunity to practice their English with a *gaijin*. The Japanese, being a shy people, used drink more than most societies to oil social situations, and the night Harry met Yoshihara was no exception. One drink led to another and another, Yoshihara insisting on pouring out continual shots of warmed sake, and so it didn't take long before they were laughing at the least comical of provocations. Yoshihara's English was halting but gaining fluency with each jigger of sake.

"Your Japanese is very good, Harry-san." Yoshihara said, when indeed it wasn't. He stumbled around with an assortment of memorized useful words and phrases. Harry returned the compliment to his new friend about his English.

"No, no, my English is very terrible."

One could safely say that all Japanese are modest people, almost to a fault, as was Yoshihara. He was quite able to provide a lot of information about himself in English that evening. He was going to be the dean of the humanities school at the new university, AUIS, and he lived near the Hara metro station, as did Harry. He wanted to know about Harry who did his best to provide a short bio in clear phrases in the style he'd practiced in the past year to better make himself understood. If only all the Japanese he encountered did the same, but it never seemed to occur to them to slow down and deliver information in clearly enunciated chunks and phrases. He was reminded of untraveled, geocentric Americans who believed they could be understood by a foreigner if they just talked louder. The evening came to an end with Yoshihara asking for Harry's phone number and he gave Harry his card. They agreed they would see each other again at the *aka-chochin* for drinks.

Harry went about his company schedule of classes and didn't see Yoshihara for weeks, until receiving a phone call from him one evening.

"Harry-san, forgive me. I have been very busy with the new school. Are you well?"

"Thank you, Yoshihara-san. I am well and you?"

"I am fine. Would you be interested in a fulltime position at our new University of International Studies?"

He knows nothing about me, Harry thought, and he's offering me a job? Talk about cutting to the chase. It was something Harry had hoped for soon after arriving in Japan. It appeared that who you knew worked wonders in Japan. He had learned how well college jobs in Japan paid and how good the benefits were with full summers off, bonuses and healthcare insurance included. Yoshihara said he would send him a fax with particulars and a map to the school.

It was all so simple and yet true, as if a job had fallen into his lap. He found out later that being in his mid-forties was an important requirement of the job in addition to academic accomplishments. Appearances were important to the Japanese. There were lots of young itinerant foreigners with degrees running around Japan, even in the 80s, but a new college had to present a degree of gravitas with a mature faculty. His only drawback was his being single. The Japanese were aware of the hazards of single male teachers having access to a lot of impressionable nubile students. Indeed, Harry would see several foreign acquaintances who taught college classes given the door for transgressions with students.

The campus was brand new with a few buildings still under construction but near completion for the fall term. He was led to the humanities building and adjoining English Department, where he was met by Yoshihara-San. Harry had brought copies of his degrees and recommendation letters from his few part-time posts he'd had in California, and his passport with his Japanese visa stamped inside. Yoshihara introduced him to Nagumo-Sensei, a white-haired senior professor, perhaps seventy, who would be heading up the department. He was warm and welcoming and spoke beautiful American English.

It appeared that Harry had already been hired because Professor Nagumo wasted no time outlined Harry's schedule of six classes for the first term.

It almost took Harry's breath away. This suddenness of his appointment was no doubt the work of Yoshihara in the background taking initiative on Harry's interest in an appointment when they spoke on the phone. Nagumo continued his job description. Harry would choose his own textbooks, and he was to put course emphasis on reading American literature with a view to learning the culture. Class time should be approximately divided between instructor lectures and student recitation. Perfect, Harry thought. This was right up his alley and would be a joy to teach.

"We expect careful evaluation of student progress. Most of your students will already have modest ability with English; that's why they are here, to acquire fluency, to get pickled, if you like, in English usage and American culture. So, balance your evaluations based on their fulfillment of assignments, both writing and verbal and their attendance to class. This is a nationally certified four-year private college with high tuition. Success of the students is paramount."

Harry liked Nagumo's choice of adjectives. *Paramount* might have many degrees, and so it remained to be seen what was truly meant. It would become an ongoing task for Harry to pin down meanings in Japan. There seemed to be an aversion to specificity, and so much communication remained *aimai*, or vague. After his conference with Nagumo, he was taken deeper into the building and the main lobby of the English Department lined with private offices. He was assigned office 103, equipped with a large desk, filing cabinet, chairs, and a splendid view of a grove of timber bamboo lining the perimeter of the building. Then he was taken to the administrative offices where he gave them copies of everything he had brought, including his passport with the stamped six-month visa. Visas would no longer have to be cow-towed for every six months once one was registered as a full-timer with a university. He was issued an insurance id card for his health coverage, a perk, and they requested his bank account number where his monthly paycheck could be deposited. They had him fill out a scant bit of personal information on a card and he was then done, officially a professor at Aichi University of International Studies.

After a marvelous celebratory dinner of all faculty from all the departments, AUIS was launched. The faculty was then requested to attend another ceremony welcoming all the new entering students. Every one of the new faculty received a signing-on welcome bonus, equal to a month's salary in gratitude for choosing to join the new school. The check was paid into his account in Japanese *yen*, the equivalent of five thousand dollars. Harry readjusted his thinking to another fifteen years in Japan with summer trips back to the U.S.

A few weeks into the kick-off term, Yoshihara met him in the lounge and struck up a conversation.

"So, Harry-sensei, what do you think?"

"Just call me Harry. I love the job, Many thanks for your support."

"*Do itashimashita.* You are part of my job. I am Dean of the Humanities, including the English Studies Department. Faculty members are my responsibility."

"I won't let you down." Harry could tell by Yoshihara's expression he didn't entirely understand.

"I will *not disappoint* you," Harry reiterated, and Yoshihara smiled.

"*Naruhodo!* I see. Soon we must drink again."

"I would like that."

"Good, let's meet at Mie-san's *aka-chochin* this evening, at 6 pm."

Checking around, Harry picked up more details about Yoshihara. He taught only two classes per semester as a dean, and he was working to write some papers for Japanese Academic journals. Harry guessed Yoshihara felt that it was incumbent on himself to lead by example. Happily, publishing was optional. The university didn't emulate American schools and universities requiring faculty to publish, but if you did, it was a feather in your cap which was rewarded with a bonus. But there was no draconian *publish or perish* maxim hanging over faculty heads like there was in American universities.

Upon inquiring, Harry found out that as long as he stayed in Japan and performed his job well, he would have tenure. How ironic, he thought, he had to come to Japan to acquire the illusive American academic dream of tenure.

That evening at Mie's bar, Harry and Yoshihara got into the sake. Harry rather liked the taste of rice wine and had a good capacity for it. It didn't leave him with the thunderous headaches he got with whisky or beer. While drinking little porcelain bottles of warmed sake poured into jigger-sized cups, they ate bite-size appetizers in between, like the Spanish eat tapas. There were small portions of sashimi, gyozas, barbequed chicken, roasted eel, and rice balls. The snacks were delicious and seemed to lessen the effects of the alcohol.

"What are your views of the war in the Pacific?"

Harry was startled at this out-of-the-blue difficult question. Yoshihara had really had too much to drink. Harry had never encountered an older Japanese who wanted to discuss WWII. Younger Japanese were all but ignorant of the war as though a nationwide amnesia had infected the country in the post war period. The only thing they could reference was the bomb. Yoshihara had such a gentle smile as he poured Harry another tiny cup of sake.

"*Muzukashii.* Isn't that what Japanese people say in a difficult or embarrassing situation?"

Harry did know a few handy expressions such as *muzukashii,* meaning hard or difficult, but he didn't add the typical Japanese tick of sucking through his teeth. He didn't want to appear to be mocking.

"Good answer. You are learning to be Japanese, but we prefer you to be American, especially at the school, yes?" Yoshihara's English was gaining fluency again per his intake of sake. Back in California that had been the effect on Harry's use of Spanish, as if the right amount of alcohol opened up the brain channel that controlled the use of a foreign language. Or maybe the alcohol just made us less self-conscious and lowered inhibition about making mistakes.

"I have mixed feelings about the bomb if that is what you are asking about, especially the second one on Nagasaki."

"Please excuse me, Harry-san, I just like having interesting conversations. In Japan, conversations among us

Japanese follow rules of politeness more than anything. It is different to exchange with foreigners, especially Americans because of your history with us, and Americans are usually more open with their opinions.

I flew a Japanese Zero fighter near the end of the war. Only a few missions. I was in the cockpit ready to take off for my last mission from an Okinawa airfield. I say last because there was not enough fuel in the plane to return to base. You know the Japanese word *Kamikaze*?"

Harry knew the story behind the *divine wind* or *kamikaze* of Japan's war with China in the 13th century and how that appellation came to be used for the suicidal pilots who crashed their planes into Allied ships for country and emperor.

"We had to die like samurai for the emperor and Japan."

"So, what happened?" Harry gave his most concerned face with knitted eyebrows.

"I was flagged down to stop the plane. And when I stopped and opened the cockpit, I was told the war had been declared over. Japan had surrendered."

"Saved by the bell, huh?"

"Saved by the bell, what bell?"

"You know, the boxing match bell that starts and stops the fighting? You were about to be finished, counted out, but the bell rang just in time, and you were saved."

"Ah, that bell, *asoka*!"

"Why are you telling me this?"

"I felt I was saved for a reason. I decided to study the West, especially America the victor. Japan had greatly underestimated the power and resolve of your country. What did Japan have to learn for all its suffering and what did I need to learn by almost dying in that plane? I was only

20 years old and so I went back to university and studied English so that I could study the great minds who made America and its culture."

"Wow! To your continued health," Harry toasted. "You are an extraordinary man, Mister Yoshihara, and I am very honored to know you," Harry said and poured a last cup of sake for each of them.

"Kampai!" They toasted and drank. The two men then talked easily about the war for another hour, until it soon became late. Yoshihara dropped a 10,000-yen bill on the bar, roughly $100, and they rolled out of Mie's, both a little unsteady but happy, and they bid each other *oyasumi nasai*, the Japanese for good night. After exchanging shallow bows, they turned toward their respective homes.

The Desert Rose

Near Needles, California off Highway 95, by the Arizona border, the desert heat was relentless. It wasn't his first time at Paul's ramshackle house on several acres with a couple ponds. The night sky full of countless stars from horizon to horizon and the silence of the desert made the place worth the visit, especially for a city dweller. Unlivable during summer, visiting the ranch in May was salutary with dry hot days in the 80s and moderate evenings in the 60s. You never really felt hot because your sweat evaporated so quickly in the dry air.

Paul Greve had been a friend ever since his pot dealing days in LA, now far behind him. Paul bought the place in the desert for a song when he got out of the dealing business which had become too hot with dark characters with strings attached to the Mexican cartels. Brad had always been supplied by Paul, so he hadn't felt any of that unwelcome heat. But when Paul got out of the business, he didn't see any alternative but to follow. The whole marijuana scene had become dirty and ugly in the few succeeding years, fraught with violence and no longer like the old days of hip young middle-class kids just looking for a little smoke and some laughs. It had become sinister.

For Brad, a little smoke now and then was okay, but a cold beer or a mellow Cabernet were now his choices, if anything at all. With a straight job like he now had in graphic design for an advertising firm, he had evolved from a lot of his younger habits. Paul, too, was a lot more sober these days and had made his ranch into a paying establishment with catfish sold to a wholesaler in LA, and organic jojoba beans to a cosmetics firm in Las Vegas where he occasionally went to play a little blackjack at the tables. He was able to maintain his simple, removed life in the desert.

When Brad needed to debrief from life in the city, he'd phone Paul to see if he was up for some company which he almost always was. The desert was a lonely place and most of the people out there were odd loners and liked it that way. Paul hadn't yet turned inward that much.

This time Brad brought his latest flame, Gina Gelashvili. Paul said he might have a sometimes girlfriend join them since Brad was bringing someone.

"Can she cook, Brad?"

"I don't really know; it's only been a while I've been dating her."

"Roxy can't cook. She's not the domestic type at all. Just as well, don't want her getting ideas about moving in and playing house."

Roxy lived and worked in Las Vegas, an hour and half drive from the house and it turned out Paul's occasional visits to Vegas were as convenient for Roxy as were her visits to his house.

"Don't you get lonely out here, Paul?"

"You know I'm a social guy, but, man, I love the solitude. When I go out at night and look up at all those stars, I feel huge and part of the universe. It's real religion, man."

Gina was tallish, slender, and dramatic looking, Brad's type. She didn't have a generic face like a department store mannikin or a Hollywood starlet. Rather she could be Eastern European with a Eurasian gene or two somewhere in the mix. He had met her at the ad agency in the front office where she typed and was the receptionist. Not the best idea to mix business with pleasure but then she was in the front reception lobby while his employee entrance was through the rear of the building from the parking lot.

She had never been out to the Californian high desert and agreed to go with him for the three-day weekend jaunt after he described Paul's place hidden away in a grove of Athel pines a quarter mile off the highway 95. Nights like you've never seen, he told her, and a swimming hole when we want to cool off.

"You do swim, I hope." She did. "And Paul is a super guy," he assured her. "Maybe his girlfriend will join us. We'll have a private wing of the house with a bathroom."

When Brad and Gina arrived at Paul's around 10:30 pm on the Friday night, Paul was out on the grounds.

"Roxy's driving out tomorrow morning. She's working tonight," he said.

"What does she do in Vegas?"

"Don't get the wrong idea but she's an exotic dancer. Not naked or anything but athletically, sometimes with a pole. She makes really good money."

Brad hoped she wouldn't be crude and would be good company for Gina who he could see reacted uncomfortably to Paul's description of Roxy.

"You guys hungry? I got some good chili and French hard rolls if you're interested."

After the four-hour drive they were hungry, and they ate small bowls so that they could sleep without their stomachs disturbing them. And then Paul showed them to their room at the back of the house with a queen bed. Everything was a little dusty, but the sheets were clean and crisp.

Paul told them if they got up early, there was instant coffee and OJ and milk in the fridge. With that he bid them goodnight and left them. Gina went to the bathroom with her full-length nightie and changed. They were exhausted and fell asleep without much ado.

The morning was cool and bright. Gina was still asleep when Brad got up, got showered and dressed and left Gina to sleep and have the room to herself. After some coffee, Brad took a walk out around the house. Schroeder, Paul's German shepherd, wagged his tail and nuzzled him, a friendly beast, and a great alarm system against unwanted intruders. The air was noticeably fresher than what he had left in LA. With each breath, he felt invigorated. He began to understand Paul's attachment to the broad, lonely expanse.

Around 10 am, they were all at the breakfast table. Brad had cooked up some eggs, bacon, and toast from the bag of basics he'd brought from LA, the least he could do. Brad was never a freeloader.

"I can't distinguish the fragrances, but everything smells so good out here," Gina said. She was bright and beautiful in her jeans and T shirt with her hair piled up on her head.

Then they heard Schroeder barking and a car pulling in. Sound traveled so clearly out in the desert. It was Roxy.

Contrary to Brad's expectations, Roxy didn't have on a speck of makeup, but then she didn't need it. She was a natural beauty with soft flowing brown hair and was well-spoken and polished. Nothing edgy about her. After greeting Paul and being introduced to everyone, she sat down next to Gina and chatted her up, entertainer that she was. Gina was happy and so was Brad. Paul announced he'd be showing everyone around the place after breakfast.

The day was still cool enough to take a casual walk around the grove of jojoba trees that Paul had cultivated. Brad noticed, without comment, the young marijuana bushes artfully camouflaged by being interspersed among the jojoba trees. Paul then took them around his two ponds, one little more than a large hole in the ground for the catfish and the other more of a natural pond with bull rushes and a mild grade from the beach-like perimeter into the deeper water fed by a spring, the swimming hole. He had three active beehives which proved that bees traveled far and wide to find the nectar they used to make honey. Gina confided to Brad how all the nature which now surrounded them made her feel relaxed in a way she hadn't felt since she couldn't remember. Better than anything one could find back in the city or at the beach; this was wild, open, free, the air pristine, dry, and clean. She too had dispensed with makeup and now sparkled.

The heat of the afternoon in addition to the feeling of having detoxed from so much clean air made everyone retire for an afternoon siesta. Brad held Gina's hand as they fell asleep in their guest room. Around 4 pm they got into their bathing suits and padded out to the swimming pond in flip flops. Brad tried not to be obvious about looking at Gina's curvaceous shape, clearly defined in her close-fitted one-piece suit. The water was warm but still cooling as they submerged to their necks. After paddling about for a while, they lay on the tiny beach with towels and watched dragonflies cavorting around the bullrushes, two of them hovering nearby, oddly stuck together. Gina's impish smile toward him acknowledged she knew what the insects were doing.

The temperature started to level off around 6 pm and so they all ventured out to the catfish pond to seine out some catfish for dinner. First, Paul threw some feed from a fifty-pound bag to bring the fish closer, and then Paul and Brad got in up to their knees in the shallow end of the pond and cast out the seine and dragged it back in with flopping and flailing black and green catfish, the biggest about a foot long. They carefully extracted four fat catfish and let the rest go back into the pond. Not experienced, Brad got punctured with a head spike when he carelessly grasped one of the fish too close to its head.

Back at the house, Gina attended to his punctured hand with some disinfectant and a band aid, while Paul made quick work of cleaning the fish, prepping them for cooking with a coat of flour and a liberal amount of Cajun spice. He put a wok on the electric stove and heated up a quart of canola oil to the right temperature so that when he slipped in the fish, they only needed to sizzle and bubble for a few minutes until browned and crisp, and then he set them aside on paper towels. He then threw in enough sliced up potatoes for everyone to have a side of fries. He produced four cold cans of Coors from the fridge, and the four happy campers toasted their good fortune on that Saturday night in the desert. They played gin rummy and listened to the Beatles until it got late. They were too spent from a day in the desert to do anything but sleep.

Having slept like rocks, everyone was up early on Sunday. They ate breakfast in the shade of the athel trees and leisurely drank coffee and chatted.

Brad was happy Gina received a lot of attention from Roxy. Brad knew Gina was enjoying her time in the desert. He gave Paul a hand making mead, mixing the right proportions of honey, water, and Brewer's yeast, and then filling and capping cleaned beer bottles, some of them exploding later during the fermentation process. Then he helped Paul repair the swinging gate across the gravel road to the property. Large rocks lining both sides of the gate, discouraged anyone from driving out and around the gate. Paul latched the gate when not around and at night to prevent entering by auto. The girls were back in the house preparing a couple lasagnas for the evening meal. Brad had brought those ingredients also, along with three bottles of imported premium Chianti for the dinner.

The lasagnas were in the oven on a slow bake and another bottle of Chianti was uncorked. Everyone was feeling good, a bit high with one bottle already finished. Roxy looked through Paul's CDs, found something she wanted and put it on the player. It was Aretha Franklin's, *Chain of Fools*, a mega-famous tune, further popularized by John Travolta's dancing to it in a movie scene with sexy women. Roxy took the stage and started out slow, a couple steps to the left, then a couple to the right, then more body into it, forward, back, side. She took Gina by the hand, inviting her to join and follow. Gina resisted at first, shy to dance in front of the men. But then bit by bit she was taken by the irresistible rhythm and beat, following Roxy's simple choreography, which she repeated until she got it. As the song progressed, Gina lost her shyness and followed Roxy's professional moves with equal undulations, gliding and panache. The women became sexier and more suggestive as the song moved on. Roxy would introduce a new move as soon as Ginna got the last one, until they put all the moves together into a refrain. They became a perfectly synched, sexy chorus line.

When the Aretha Franklin piece wound down, ending their dance, Brad and Paul gave them whistles, hoots and a long, loud applause. Gina, red-faced, trotted back to where she had been sitting, too embarrassed to respond to the applause. It was as if she had been enticed and revealed by Roxy. Under that reserved exterior, Gina was a talented dancer and proved bigger than the natural inhibition that restrains most people. Or perhaps it was just the wine.

"Honey, if you should ever need a job, come and see me, you hear?" Roxy said. "How about this girl?" she addressed the men who applauded a second time.

If she had that talented dance ability in her, Brad thought, what else might she be capable of? She no doubt had other talents that just needed to be brought out. He didn't know her, but he then resolved to know her better.

Roxy refilled her own glass and then went to Gina and refilled hers.

"Did you know, Brad, that this young lady is trained in classical ballet?" Roxy queried.

"You ladies have been talking a lot. Did you know that about Gina?" Paul said, looking at Brad with disbelief.

"Wow, ballet? You never mentioned anything, Gina."

"I was never quite good enough," she said, sipping her Chianti.

"She could be a headliner at the Crazy Horse, believe me." Roxy said.

"Brad, I think the lasagnas are done now. What do you say, ladies?" Paul addressed the women, who started for the kitchen.

"No, no, wait a minute," Brad intervened. "I'll do it."

He took the casseroles from the oven and put them on the table, called the ladies to the table, seated each of them, served their plates, and then topped off their wine glasses. They deserved special treatment. It was the best lasagna he'd ever eaten.

That night, when the lights were out and they were in bed, Brad gently kissed Gina with a tenderness he had just discovered in himself. She touched his face lightly with her fingertips, looked deeply into his eyes in the half light and thanked him for such a wonderful weekend. Wine and an active day in the desert air had taken their effect on them. She cuddled up to him and whispered into his ear. "I will cook special for you tomorrow, sweet man."

Rigatoni Blues

had to remind my brother that many families were split by the Civil War. And when things got bad in Germany, some families split up over Hitler. The smart ones, especially the Jews, got the hell out! Not an option for me and Eva. Besides I didn't believe Trump and his advocates were going to get very far.

I had been fighting with my family back East for more than twenty years. First it was about Bush, then Obama and finally about Trump. We tried to find common ground to no avail. But they believed we had common ground enough simply because of our family blood. I didn't want to fight but I couldn't remain quiet when my brother Carl and my sister Talia would drop rightwing bombs. They were dear to me, but they took a wrong turn over the years. I mean if the grandparents from Italy were alive, they'd be disgusted how their grandchildren had drifted. The old generation were all Democrats and hard-working union people, four generations in Buffalo, New York.

Uncle Manny liked to recount his experiences on picket lines and the fistfights he had with scabs. A fierce union man, he was proud of his part in acquiring a decent wage for steel workers, from the lowest in the foundries to those working on drawing board in offices. Brother Carl would not be ignorantly bad-mouthing labor were Uncle Manny still around, at least not in his presence. Grandma Julietta, who came through Ellis Island, and became a suffragette in her day, would not have stood for Talia's support of so-called pro-life anti-abortionists, even though Julietta claimed to be a good Catholic.

I guessed my Buffalo family got their brains washed when they took over an In-N-Out Burger franchise, which I came to refer to as the F-burger, not appreciated by Carl and Talia. Not long after high school Carlo went into the burger business and eventually took over a franchise where he took in Talia who was floundering in retail jobs. This was a company whose corporate leaders started off meetings with solemn prayer. My brother and sister soon became hard-working Christian soldiers, followers of Bush and finally of Trump with his Make America Great Again narrative.

Their most recent email included several photos with a short message wishing me and Eva a joyful summer. They used the word *joy* frequently.

The photos were of a gathering of Esposito cousins from around the state and tables laden with large serving dishes of Italian specialties: Gnocchi with pesto, eggplant parmesan, and Rigatoni a la marinara, food I had grown up with, made by our mother, no longer with us along with our father. The occasion was Carl's retirement from In-N-Out Burger with whom he'd bought two more franchise locations over the years. He and his wife Lola were selling their house in Buffalo and moving to Florida, where there were Esposito cousins. My sister Talia had long ago left In-N-Out Burger for housekeeping as the wife of Bill Califano, an assemblyman from the red suburb of Williamsville.

I saw their email as caviling with me for not being a part of our family traditions which they still carried on with exuberance, my mother's cooking, and the *familia* thing ad nauseam. One of our last phone exchanges I'd had with Carl was just after the invasion of Iraq.

"What happened to *never again* after Viet Nam?" I asked.

"We should have won that one."

"Come on, Carlo, be real."

"We should have doubled-down and brought in bigger guns."

"Like we didn't drop enough bombs on the North?"

"All right, all right, Rick. But now is now."

"It's just about the oil, Carlo. Don't you get it?"

"When there's a bully on the block like Saddam, we got to act, right?"

"Wrong."

That was the extent of that exchange and there has been little since, awkwardly reserved and perfunctory. When Obama was elected and phenomenal hope flooded the country, the haters and bigots came out of the woodwork with equal enthusiasm. Obama was born in Africa, an unacknowledged son of Malcom X, was a Muslim, caused the recession of 1995 and wanted to make us a socialist country. The last crazy idea had deep resonance with Carl and Talia. They both had golden health insurance and it never occurred to them that millions went without in our great country, that Obama Care was about as socialist as the Buffalo School district and post office.

Talia continued to send emails loaded with family gathering photos with people from the far-reaching Esposito family that had originated from Naples. It may have been mildly charming in a nostalgic way before we had all entered into a polarized era. I think both Carl and Talia genuinely were attached to our family history, the food and family gatherings, but they insisted on no real talk. My wife Eva had just said enough was enough to Talia. There was no getting by their cockamamy beliefs, no getting by with talk of family when the future of the planet and voting rights were on the table. They said they didn't vote for Trump but then who did they vote for? Certainly not Hillary who, according to their popular conspiracy mills, was running a pedophile trafficking ring out of a pizza shop. They wouldn't talk about anything, probably because none of them could. I had already found out from Carl that any suggestion they were ignorant infuriated them, as if their regurgitations from Rush Limbaugh and chat rooms were bona fide facts. They didn't want to face the hard reality that there were no such thing as alternative facts. But they were tenacious in their professed love of us by sending every photo-op of every Esposito gathering they could. This was their rejoinder to the faux MAGA reality which they avoided discussing.

The Covid 19 pandemic that brought the Trump era to an ugly close didn't dampen Carl's or Talia's die-hard support for him and the Republican Party. They bought into the hoax theory and refused to get a vaccination. Thank God, they didn't buy the bleach cure rumor.

"We're taking all the immune boosters we can and wearing masks. We don't trust the vaccine," Talia said, throwing down a glove.

"Okay, Madam Curie, you got it all figured out…excuse me, you wouldn't know who she was. Anyway, I don't want to have to run back to Buffalo because you've been intubated to a ventilator."

"You were always a smart ass, Rick, even as a kid."

"But this isn't a joke, sis!"

"When are you ever going to respect my point of view?"

"Your point of view on vaccination? Never!"

That was the end of that exchange. I was sorry that we were on different sides of reason and science, but it seemed there were many people like my brother and sister, that the country's sorry polarization, even among families, was being repeated like it had been during the Civil War, the deep South again being a main location of resolute detraction from reason and a moral compass.

Am I wrong here? Should I be able to put aside politics for the sake of family harmony? There was a time when the aisle between the parties wasn't so wide, certainly back in the 60s when so much social legislation was passed. Now the Republicans don't want to hear about anything that doesn't cut taxes or bolster their power at the polls. Hasn't it been the Republicans who've pulled further to the right, making the aisle wider and the Democrats look more left?

There must come a time when we stand our ground and be honest. If we relent for the sake of false peace, we become part of the problem and it continues unaddressed. If those we love are wrong, we have to call them out.

In addition to the photos of Italian feasts, there was their often-stated sanctimony that they would pray for me and Eva. Or Talia would signoff in her emails with *God bless*. I got that sort of thing whenever I dropped off some loose change to a homeless panhandler at a street corner. All the blessing and praying everywhere but no sanity. Everyone was entreated to pray for near daily new shooting victims and their families, but no gun control legislation gained traction in Congress. The insurrection against Congress in January 2021 was being called a demonstration by some members of Congress, and the valid election of Joe Biden a fraud. The extremes had gathered storm proportions which made me more likely to reject the blandishments of my

Russ Desaulnier

family who were part of the problem. Little did Carl and Talia know about how it hurt me. They acted as if I didn't care about them.

"You don't love your family anymore. I feel sorry for you," Talia pronounced over the phone.

"You just don't get it, Talia. I'm sorry too."

I remembered all her stages in life, the sweet child, the flippant high schooler, her struggles and victories, her marriage to her ambitious boyfriend Bill Califano.

It was the summer of 2021, six months after the insurrection, and the country was suffering biblical storms and floods, fires and heat waves, while madman Trump was still lingering in the wings, yammering about his stolen election, when I got an email from Lola telling me that Carl had been arrested by the Feds. They had come to the house with an arrest warrant for his part in the march against Congress in January!

This took my breath away. The absolute fool, my brother, I thought. Yes, all the signs were there, but I never imagined my brother would join in an insurrection. Maybe Carlo really thought it would be just a *march*. Rick knew Lola his wife knew. Didn't she call the violent insurrection a march? Undoubtedly, there were some people among the mob who didn't expect the violence. Wasn't the same true for marches on the left where instigators have broken windows and torched cars, bringing the police down on everyone with a heavy hand?

Despite feeling hesitance, I called my sister. I felt no desire to gloat. Somehow the seriousness of the situation had leveled everything down to our blood connection. This could mean prison time for Carlo. At the very least, Carl's and Lola's move to Florida would have to be postponed.

"Does Bill know about this?" I began.

"Not yet."

"There's really nothing I can do. I think you ought to let Bill know about this. He may be able to do something. I mean, he knows people in politics who might be able to pull a string or two. But then no one's above the law. What in the hell was Carlo thinking anyway?"

"Carl just said it was going to be a peaceful protest march and he was simply going, you know, for solidarity with a few of his pals here in Buffalo. He insisted. That's you Esposito men, stubborn as hell."

"No, it had nothing to do with stubborn, just stupidity. Sorry, Talia. Surely you didn't expect me to be sympathetic."

Carlo had always been a mercurial kid, quick to do inadvisable things, like jumping off a second story onto a sand pile thinking it would cushion the fall. Drag racing as a teenager got his license pulled. It was a miracle he and Lola stayed married for so many years when everyone knew they got married just after high school because she was pregnant, that first child followed by three more daughters. I always got the obligatory family photo Christmas card every year with Carlo surrounded by all his pretty women, quite a picture when all his girls were grown up and Lola still a looker with her graying long hair and preserved figure. There wasn't a peep from Talia. I expected she felt too much egg on her face. I hoped her husband Califano, would be able to pull some strings, if the charges weren't severe, that Carlo would get off with some community service, probation, or fines.

I received an email from Lola a month later telling me that Carl had been released with a sentence of three months of Community Service, assigned to a task force to get Americans vaccinated, which possibly could have Carlo going door to door with a health worker to offer shots. A painless just dessert, I thought, and appropriately ironic for someone who had so vehemently opposed Biden and believed the election was a fraud.

My mother would be happy that Carlo got off lightly, although she would have twisted his cheek for being such a fool. Apparently, his participation in the insurrection was as I had guessed, minimal. His face had been caught on a video taken out on the grounds in front of the Congressional building, and not inside. In the photo he'd not been carrying anything that looked like a weapon, but he did have on his red MAGA hat. His attorney had plea-bargained that Carl had believed it was going to be a peaceful march and not what it turned into, and he did not participate in any melee with the police and did not enter the building nor destroy any property.

Remembering my mother, I recalled the sumptuous Italian meals she prepared. All the recent family involvement brought back memories of my family dinners with a huge Rigatoni casserole set in the middle of the table, I and my two siblings anxious to dive in, my mother beaming at her growing children, my father, stern and stalwart at the head of the table, preparing to say grace.

"Hey, Eva, you got any Rigatoni in the pantry?"

The Bachelor

He had a small two-bedroom shack in Santa Barbara about three blocks from the beach and thirty yards from the Pacific railroad track. The little house tremored with the night trains, but he could sleep through anything in those days. He could see Ruth and Roger's breakfast house out his kitchen window and the plain stucco front of Little Athens, the Greek restaurant and night club. Directly across the street, he could watch the comings and goings at the neighborhood liquor store. Just around the corner out of sight was Aiello's market where he kept a tab. He lived there four years, the usual time it takes to get a BA degree at a liberal arts college. You might say his time at that shack was an education, the convergence of Bath and Montecito Streets his world.

It was during his time there that Mark made the slow break-up from the woman who, up until that time, had been the most momentous romance in his life. He was lucky to have landed in the shack where his lifeline took a turn upward and the wound of his separation from Veronica was quick to heal. She was beautiful and tragic like the Veronica pass performed by the best bullfighters in Madrid, a slow flowing of magenta and gold cloth leading a sharp horn only inches from a thigh and its mortal femoral artery, exquisite scary beauty.

Nicholas Vitalis, just Nick to everyone at the Little Athens club, was a handsome middle-aged man, who like his name, had the vitality of a younger man. Six nights a week, he was the force and spirit at the club until midnight. For about a year Mark was a regular at the club, having become an expert Greek dancer and connoisseur of Greek retsina wines. He studied the movie *Zorba* until he was able to lead or follow the Sirtaki dance which, after having performed it once successfully with master Nick, he occasionally got called upon to perform the iconic dance with him. He guessed that Nick's nightly dancing was how he kept in shape, his fine physique emphasized by his clingy fitted shirts and tailored slacks.

For a single man always on the lookout for female companionship, Little Athens was a gold mine. There was always an assortment of young women, often tipsy with drink, happy and friendly. They usually came to the club in pairs for a night out. Those pairings were the best bet. With his acquired dancing expertise, Mark had the perfect introduction, and he used it, asking whoever he liked to join him in the line of dance, arms on shoulders, sometimes as many as twelve dancers, all the way up to the lead, Nick the Greek. The good time of it all made friends of everyone at the club.

With this routine of the Greek dancing, Mark met a slender, small-featured woman with translucent, azure eyes. She responded to his attentions after a few dances, and he made a walk-picnic-date with her for the beach. The great beauty of Santa Barbara was its beaches and countryside, especially up the coast a few miles, perfect for pastoral dates. Natalie was not long divorced and had a girl of four, which he found out on their stroll up Refugio Beach. After they got back to Santa Barbara, Natalie asked him to stop by and pick up her daughter from her ex-husband. Mark waited in the car while she approached a shacky bungalow like his. The ex-husband looked as though he'd just flown in from the San Francisco Haight—scruffy beard, shirtless and barefoot, lots of curly hair and several strands of beads around his neck. Mark drove Natalie and her little Leslie back to her co-housing in a vintage rambling house on Ortega Street and dropped her off. After Veronica, Mark was shy of mothers with small children. He didn't want to take on the surrogate daddy role again, double trouble. Despite Natalie being a wonderful dancer, even Flamenco in her repertoire, he backed away from her. After Veronica, he didn't want any more similar entanglements.

One night at the Little Athenas, he took up the challenge of the table dance. Familiar with him, Nick was willing to give Mark a go. The dance consisted of dancing with a light card-sized table clenched in one's mouth and teeth and the table counter-balanced with a table leg against one's torso. Mark pulled it off with a smooth dance to the slow Greek ballad which he'd learned from having watched Nick so many times. He didn't realize the price of this bit of exhibitionism until the next morning when his neck felt frozen in muscular agony. His neck muscles had tightened to board like stiffness. It took him almost a week to get back to normal, pain-free flexibility.

During his recovery time and a break from his carousing, change came Mark's way in the form of his 19-year-old cousin Jeanie who showed up at his door with a small suitcase. She needed to make a change from Los Angeles and family. Of course, he would be glad of the company, and he had an extra room, however small. She would work and contribute to the pantry which mainly consisted of simple quesadillas and pasta. Sometimes for a change they would go out and eat at Franks Rice Bowl on lower State St., the cheapest Chinese in town.

He'd known Jeanie since she was a baby when he was fifteen and just arrived in Southern California from back East with his parents. He watched her grow through the years in visits to her family, his uncle and aunt. He had history with her. She made him think of his uncle Ernie who'd taught him how to play golf as a boy. Jeanie was mum about her parents, but he imagined Uncle Ernie was concerned for her as any father would be, although there was no conferring. Jeanie had cut the rope for the time being. Was uncle Ernie possibly wondering what Jeanie was up to living with his older brother's over-grown child, the beach bum running around Santa Barbara in a jalopy sports car?

The back room was small but had a single bed that doubled as a couch. Mark had some single sheets and a blanket, so he was able to set her up. He was still on unemployment insurance, but he always had enough for food, and so the first thing he did was go to Aiello's and get in groceries to make some real meals for his skinny little cousin. He gave her one of his little electric fans in case they hit some extra hot weather.

"I just had to get out of LA. You know how it is." She was so grateful to have landed in his drafty little shack, he couldn't hide his embarrassment.

"I don't imagine my uncle Ernie is happy about this," he replied.

"I also had to get away from a relationship."

"Now you're talking my language, Sweetie. Me too."

"I really liked this guy, and my mom was pushing it, but I just didn't want to get married so young and start the whole housewife thing."

"Hell, I know—house, spouse, child, the full catastrophe! as Zorba the Greek put it in the movie."

That night when he went to bed after he'd got her settled, the few things she'd brought put away in a small chest of drawers in the extra room, he lay awake, wondering what he was going to do with this girl who fate had dropped into his life.

The mornings became something new and lovely. Up early without hangovers for a change, he would make toast and coffee and they'd stand around the little kitchen and watch the early stirrings at the liquor shop across the street. That was their morning show which inspired their inventing stories about the shabby characters who went in and out of the store with paper bagged bottles of booze, probably pints of sherry or Old Southern Rye whiskey.

Mark found her full of good humor with a ready laugh. After a few days, she was out the door and looking for work. He began to feel the place needed some changes, for starters, a good source of heat for the winter just around the corner. It sometimes got cold that close to the beach. He started that project by purchasing a fifty-gallon drum at a recycle center and had a welder friend make cuts to the drum for the opening and the chimney pipe and weld on the bottom four legs for it to sit on a pad of bricks. It still wasn't too late to plant a summer garden which he accomplished with cucumber starters, later to become pickles in a large crock bought at a flea market. Jeanie helped by planting some partially grown tomatoes.

Mark had helped a doctor friend move a dozen beehives from his avocado grove in north town, and so he gave Mark a hive and some spare beekeeping equipment and fifty dollars as compensation. He installed the hive on the sunny side of the shack, but he would be the sole caretaker of that hobby without Jeanie. He took her to his local hardware store and had her pick out some paint for her room. Then they went to Pier 1 and bought her a lamp, and a few odds and ends needed for the kitchen. At a nearby nursery, he bought three Staghorn ferns to dress up the living room. The ferns did well in Santa Barbara's climate. He had three light-weight Indian tapestries left over from his San Francisco days which they hung for added décor. He got out his old barely used cookbooks and started trying interesting but economical meals for them. He experimented with a few off-beat dishes like Peruvian *anticuchos*, cubes of beef heart marinated in beer and tarragon and skewered for grilling; chicken stir fry was also cheap and easy to make, and of course, a dozen different variations on the quesadilla.

He hadn't thought of Veronica for weeks. He finally felt he had cleansed and cured himself of the last remnants of that relationship that had lasted six years. Jeanie had been with him for almost a month when he realized he had barely had anything to drink and hadn't visited Little Athens and didn't miss it. The table dance had perhaps cured him. Jeanie had painted her room a lovely pale yellow and she helped him redecorate the shack, room by room with fresh paint. He cleaned up his bedroom cum-study space and Jeanie helped him repaint it. He had also begun some new sculptures in wax that he thought he might cast in bronze if he ever had the extra money to do so. He caught up on his neglected correspondences and even wrote and sent some warm sentiments to his mother and father with whom he'd had little contact in the last few months. He asked them to tell Uncle Ernie, if they saw him, that Jeanie was fine and thriving in Santa Barbara. Their garden of cucumbers and late tomatoes were growing fine. Jeanie had found a part-time job waitressing at Maggie McFly's, a decent restaurant and bar downtown on State St. She was taking good care of herself, and she was growing up before his very eyes. Chance had brought him a delightful sister.

They lived privately, except for mornings when they convened at the kitchen window, their morning television with coffee, but mostly she stayed to herself, often absorbed in big novels like those of James Michener. And that was fine with Mark. She was a smart young woman and had signed up for a few classes at the nearby junior college. Not long after he had sent the letter to his parents, Jeanie received a check in the mail from Uncle Ernie instructing her to get a cheap car. One couldn't live without wheels—always true in California.

Their rooms were the opposing points of a right-angle triangle with the kitchen and bathroom intervening in between at the corner. He didn't bother her, and she didn't bother him. The bathroom having two separate entrances, they had to remember to latch the doors when in use. He let Jeanie pick the paint colors for the bathroom and kitchen to suit her own taste. The shack became a sweet little home.

After six months, Jeannie went to work fulltime for Safeway and was trained as a checker. He saw less of her, but he had plenty to fill his time. He had taken up Hatha Yoga at the East Beach pavilion and could get through a week on one pack of Marlboros. He had become lean, flexible, and tanned and he was swimming. He felt he had become youngish again.

One Friday night in late winter, he had the oil drum fireplace crackling with a small fire that kept their little house warm despite its thin walls, and he had cooked up some Thresher shark steaks under the broiler and made some home fries and salad to accompany the fish, one of a variety they often bought at wholesale prices from John the fisherman, a local guy who pedaled his catches direct to the house. Mark allowed himself one glass of white wine with this splendid dinner, as did Jeanie.

They had almost finished the dinner when Jeannie announced she was engaged to get married. In fact, before the month was over, she would be pulling up stakes to move in with her fiancée Bix, a name Mark had only heard in passing conversations. He hadn't fully absorbed the implications of this news while he questioned her decision. She was just twenty years old and although the wedding wasn't planned until she turned 21 in six months, tying the knot seemed premature. She was just getting started in life, hadn't been through college and had no career potential. Old fashioned, her mother apparently was all for the engagement.

"Would it hurt to wait a bit?" he insisted, wondering how much she felt pressured. "You don't have to feel pressure from me. You can stay here as long as you want."

"I know and I'm grateful, but I think moving in with Bix will work."

"Okay, but wasn't an early marriage and doing the whole housewife number one of the reasons you got away from the boyfriend and LA?" I queried. I was confused, or I was feeling the first emotional impact of my impending solitude in the shack once again.

"Bix will support me while I go to school."

Of course, she didn't expect his largesse to reach that far. Bix did have a thriving property management business and owned a house in town. By all accounts, he was no slouch. There was no arguing with her wanting to finish a college education; marriage or not, she'd have something at the end of the day.

Two weeks after Jeanie's announcement, she moved in with Bix up on Pedregosa St. near De La Vina into a modest little Spanish stucco bungalow. Mark had been married young when he was 22, and so it was not a big surprise he divorced two years later, before he even graduated college. He had to concede that perhaps women were more mature and wiser for their years than men. That same week after visiting Jeanie's new house, Mark relented and drove to Little Athens for the happy hour.

Foreigner Sickness

Frank dubbed his recurring headaches ice pick attacks to describe the piercing, throbbing pain in his head. There were only two things he could do to lessen the pain: keep still and take hot baths. The headaches were usually unpredictable, but sometimes if he woke up feeling heavy, it was a sign that as the day progressed, he would develop one of his ice picks. Fortunately, the university classes he taught were in the mornings. He hadn't had to call in sick yet.

Only when nothing worked, sometimes not even the baths, he would take one of Dr. Hirano's prescriptions for pain. Dr. Hirano was a good, caring man and had told him not to take the prescription unless nothing else worked. He'd warned Frank they could be habit forming. Meanwhile, he went through a battery of cat-scans of his head that showed no abnormalities. Dr. Hirano also gave him a tranquilizer called Wypax with advice to try them to help him sleep. After the cat-scans, Dr. Hirano speculated his problem was simply stress that brought on a tightening of muscles in the neck and shoulders. The pills did help Frank with sleep but left him feeling hung over the next day.

"At the end of the day, which you Americans like to say, you have foreigner's sickness, *gaijin byo*, a stress induced illness that can manifest itself in various ways, commonly in headaches such as you have," Dr. Hirano declared.

Hirano was not only fluent in English but articulate, befitting his status as a downtown doctor. Thirty years with an American missionary wife had indeed made him almost bi-cultural, as well as bilingual. It was no surprise that his practice served a great many English-speaking foreigners in Nagoya.

"Frank-san, I'm going to suggest you get more exercise, especially stretching your body to relieve tension. It's not every person's cup of tea, but I am also going to suggest meditation. It may do you good more than the pills I've prescribed," he explained, handing him a business card from his desk drawer. The card was printed in Japanese on one side and in English on the other: Ito Hideyuki, Zen Master, Osu Kannon Buddhist Temple, Nagoya, Japan.

Frank noted the doctor's self-satisfaction in using the cup-of-tea expression and thought about the card in his hand. Osu Kannon was a place he loved and had frequented over the years for its *itchi*, or weekend flea market. In the middle of downtown, Osu Kannon was a large wooden structure painted red and white with broad open grounds in front of the temple building. At the Sunday *itchi* held there, one could find everything from used kimonos to antique samurai swords valued at thousands of dollars. Frank fancied the blue and white Chinese style porcelains, especially those featuring scenes with ancient characters in traditional garb. Over the years, he'd purchased a small collection of these delicate vases and pots. They were a luxury he afforded himself because he wanted something special that would recall his years in Japan when he was again in the States in the future, a memory stone.

The next time he went to the *ichi,* he would see if the Zen master was about. The temple was always open just like churches in the West, with the scent of incense lingering as it does in some Roman Catholic churches. He was beyond religion at 49, but he had some interests in Zen, having read Alan Watts in his college days. No harm in checking out the Master.

He had barely entered the temple grounds through a huge Torii gate when across the yard his eyes were drawn to a watermelon sized, blue and white pot on a pedestal, probably once a ginger jar, adorned with a superb painting of a Chinese dragon that encircled the circumference. He had to have it and made a beeline to the seller's spot. *Yon Man* in Japanese yen, or approximately four hundred dollars, was the price after some haggling with the seller. It didn't have a maker's *hanko* stamp on the bottom, but it was old, most likely nineteenth century and in fine condition with no chips or cracks. No matter the expensive indulgence, he'd cut back elsewhere in the coming monthly budgets. The pot would someday be a center piece in his eventual home where he'd grow old and remember Japan.

The pot was an armful wrapped in newspaper. He was elated that he'd got it before some other collector with similar taste had grabbed it. He thought he had better get it back to his apartment carefully. Carrying around a fragile heirloom in crowded Japan was not recommended. But since he was already at the temple and felt expansive with his purchase, he decided to see if the Zen Master was available. Most Japanese paused at the entrance of the temple proper and lit incense sticks and stuck them into large brass urns filled with sand and then held their hands together and bowed their heads in prayer. There were only several people in the red carpeted main altar area of the temple where Frank approached a temple employee and handed him the business card, explaining in Japanese he wanted to see the *roshii*, the Master. He took the card and disappeared behind the heavy curtain enclosing the altar room and large golden Buddha.

Moments later, the master appeared in saffron robes, exiting from behind the curtains. Of modest stature like most middle-aged Japanese men, his head was shaved, and he carried a fixed expression of pleasure or mild amusement. He bowed ceremoniously to Frank who bowed back and began mumbling an introduction of himself in labored Japanese when the master interrupted.

"You can speak in English with me Frank-san."

Frank had forgotten that the business card was in English as well as Japanese.

"Yes, of course. I was recommended to you by Doctor Hirano."

"Ah so, how is the good doctor? Fine, I hope."

"Yes, he sends his regards."

"He said you teach meditation."

"I only show the way. It is up to the student to persevere. When I was told there was a *gaijin* wanting to see me, I brought this schedule in English for you."

Frank couldn't decide then. He would have to compare his university schedule with the schedule of meditation sessions. He noted that many sessions were held at 3 am at the temple. Was that part of the discipline?

"How much do the sessions cost? I see nothing here on the schedule about fees."

"There is no charge," the Master said, his expression of amusement intensifying. "Students donate to the temple according to their ability."

Frank thought their arrangement no different from the average church back home: the proverbial hat was passed.

"I will give the schedule some consideration, Sensei."

"Very good, Frank-san. Please come when you are ready," the master said, in a warmly inflected tone, and then without any further hesitation, he bowed, about-faced and left Frank standing where he'd waited in front of the golden Buddha.

On the subway trip back home, he got a seat and held the pot with a firm grip on his lap. Once in his tiny apartment, Frank placed the new acquisition among others on his special bookcase reserved for his collected porcelains. The new dragon piece, with its white areas bearing fine lines like cracks called *raku,* didn't feel like an extravagant purchase but like a life achievement. It would be a joy forever.

Classes went extraordinarily well that week and not one ice pick to the head. He had his classes reading Raymond Carver's *What We Talk About When We Talk About Love,* and he gave them short quizzes with multiple choice questions to evaluate reading comprehension. Everyone passed as he'd hoped in their reading of Carver's economical prose. The question on themes and discussion of cultural phenomena was a bit more difficult. But Frank got them talking. Japanese students, usually reserved, were almost as anxious to express themselves about love as were American students. Weren't the young everywhere preoccupied by their raging hormones, though usually lacking in experience?

Swimming he discovered made his headaches less frequent. He found the buoyancy of water relaxed him and improved his sleep. He cut back his coffee consumption and found a Shiatsu sensei to work him over bimonthly. He was taking less Wypax and drinking less alcohol. Although drink relaxed him, it sometimes disturbed his sleep. Besides, he wanted all the clarity he could muster. His headaches could sometimes leave him with brain fog. His number of pool laps at his athletic club increased to thirty within a few weeks, and so he had shelved the idea of Zen meditation at Osu Kannon with the Master. The pool was on the way back home from the university, whereas the temple and Zen sessions required a long Metro ride into town and back. What is more, he wasn't about to sit in any meditation sessions at the temple at 3 am.

Frank had one of his periodic get-togethers with Brian Meadows and Howard Ramsey at The Elephant's Nest, an English style Pub near Fushimi Station downtown. Both homesick for England, they indulged in multiple pints of ale and greasy British snacks like bangers. Frank nursed a couple of weak gin & tonics all evening. Occasionally, he just had to let go with a few drinks. Beer just bloated him and laid heavy on him, whereas the gin & tonic induced highs that faded gradually and left him with no aftermath when he followed up with enough food. He could sleep well on a little gin. Frank could see that Meadows was slipping into alcoholism, if not there already, and Howard was headed for yet more weight and possibly diabetes if he didn't put the brakes on his food consumption. Frank saw his friends' excesses like his headaches, the results of living in Japan, self-medication for lives that were essentially isolated and lonely. They were called *kuchisabishii* in Japanese, lonely mouths. Living in a place as radically foreign as Japan was difficult, like the language, for almost every Westerner Frank had met. People got a little crazed and needed something to help. Some chose booze and food.

April and cherry blossom time came around again, that Japanese season of festivities and kimonos which was the most touted portrayal of the country, as if the seasons never revolved, that it was always spring gorgeous. Years had begun to stack up for Frank without his taking stock of where he was going, other than toward more age. He couldn't decide on an exit strategy from Japan. Where would he resettle in the States? Was he ever going to have a partner? A family? Did he need one?

Then the big earthquake came during a class at the university. He was making some notes on the blackboard when the room started shifting and then made some big shakes. Students were hanging on to their desks and shrieking. Frank put his hands down on his desk for support and then the desk moved under his hands. The shaking continued for a minute and then paused for a breathtaking thirty seconds until another aftershock dislodged more furniture and shattered some glass from the classroom windows that looked out across the city.

Everyone, including him, had frozen where they were until it was apparent the quake had run its course. Considering the shocked state of the students and broken glass on the floor, he adjourned the class and told them to step carefully on the way out.

When he arrived back to the department lounge and his office, a front office employee was making the rounds telling him and others that the school would be closed for several days while repairs were being made. His office was a mess with a bookcase that had fallen forward and spewed books all over the floor. Then Frank remembered his porcelain collection.

He raced home in his clunky vintage Toyota and up the five flights of stairs to his apartment. Out of breath, he blew through the door. What he feared most had happened. The bookcase with the porcelain had not withstood the quake, a neat 6, not the worst on the Richter scale but long in aftershocks. His prized vases and pots lay strewn across the floor. Although their fall was cushioned by the *tatami* mats, they had broken by contact with each other in the fall, and the bookcase coming down on top finished off the destruction. Of fifteen pieces, eight were grievously fractured and three were broken into pieces, including his recent acquisition, the big dragon ginger jar.

He shouted an obscenity at the top of his lungs. These pieces were to be the legacy of his time in Japan. Now rubble, they represented so many trips to the *itchi,* ten years of collecting porcelain in Nagoya. He had never dreamed that such a thing would happen, or he would have better secured his display case or used a better one.

He'd saved a good amount at Citibank, but he couldn't leave Japan yet because he hadn't saved near enough to retire, which didn't seem feasible until he was 60. Not only that, but he still didn't know where to resettle back in the States. He knew he couldn't bring himself to start collecting porcelain again, trying to replace the irreplaceable. That would be too depressing. He had to find some resolution to the miasma of feelings that possessed him. It was as if every little anger he had held back over his years in Japan had suddenly snowballed into a pulsating bomb in his gut. He felt the beginning of one of his piercing headaches, and so he relented and took a Wypax. He would probably feel washed out like a wet rag tomorrow, but at least he'd be able to sleep. In his distracted state, he couldn't bear to see any of his friends. He knew he was in a funk, accepted it and allowed himself to wallow in feeling sorry for himself.

With the university closed for a week in the aftermath of the earthquake, Frank just lay around his tiny apartment and binged on videos and junk food. Finally, after two list-less days, he gradually stirred himself, checked the Roshii's meditation schedule and took the subway downtown to Osu Kannon Temple.

The Bavarian Garden 1975

n Long Beach, California decades ago, there was a beer
hall and restaurant called the Bavarian Garden on 7th St.
about two miles west of the University. The owners Gisela
and Gerhardt were from the old country, late middle-aged
and a kind, out-going sort whom patrons loved. They still
had their German accents and they made authentic German
dishes. In fact, Thursday evenings always featured Gisela's
homemade sauerbraten, whipped mashed potatoes and her
tangy gravy at a bargain price that brought a lot of us from
the university crowd.

I was teaching four classes part-time at Long Beach
State University, Freshman Composition and American
Literature 101, and I had begun the Master of Fine Arts
program at UC Irvine a short ride down the coast, hoping
to write a novel for the degree. I had been at the course work
for a year and hoped to finish in no more than two more.
Meanwhile my part time teaching was solid and might turn
into fulltime with my acquisition of the MFA, at that time
a relatively new terminal degree as an alternative to a PhD.

For some of us untenured instructors and grad students,
the Bavarian Garden was a popular hangout, Gerhardt and
Gisela like family. We not only came for the dinner specials
but also for a tapped beer or two in the late afternoons after
classes. My pal Ralph E., also a part-timer and working

on an MFA, got Gerhardt's okay for holding a bi-monthly poetry reading in the bar part of the establishment with the provision that all attendees would be of drinking age. That left out most underclassmen, but Ralph E. was more interested in those of age anyway, especially the women. I had also been on the outlook for a lady friend for some time when I met Pilar O'Brien, an English major with a history minor, who wrote a little poetry on the side and liked a little beer now and then. It was her first time at Ralph-E's poetry reading. She was hip to poetry, whereas I was more an enthusiast of prose, the novel and short story. The only poets I knew anything about were W. H. Auden, W. B. Yeats, and some T.S. Eliot. I immediately picked up on Pilar's name and asked if her parents were Hemingway fans and decided on the name of his strong gypsy woman in *For Whom the Bell Tolls*. Wonderfully coincidental, I was right (or she played along) about the parents and that locked us in for the evening with head-to-head conversation over several Pilseners. She was just finishing up her MA work at the Long Beach campus and hoped to find a teaching job somewhere after graduation.

She was a real Irish looker in my book, petite with just enough sense of irony to be fun and not off-putting. She was quick to laugh, easy going and engaging—and attractively dressed above the down-dressed lot who frequented the poetry gatherings, some looking homeless in their ragged clothing. Ralph E. was the high priest of these Fridays with his rimless bespeckled John Lennon looks. Gisela and Gerhardt kept their prices competitive and so they sold a lot of tapped beer from the bar in sturdy handled mugs. The bar, like the dining room, was ringed by tendrils of fake ivy vines and a ledge that held a lineup of old ornate German beer steins. The walls were knotty pine decorated with framed posters of German landmarks—the Reichstag, the Brandenburg Gate, The Neuschwanstein castle, the Cologne Cathedral, etc. I had two semesters of German in my freshman year when I thought I was going to be pre-med, but that changed in my sophomore year after a round of reading Irwin Shaw, Mailer and Hemingway.

"So, what's your plan now?" Pilar was asking.

"To have another Pilsner and get to know you more."

"So, you want to be a standup comedian, is that it?"

"I have to write a novel."

"Everyone I meet is writing a novel or a collection of poetry."

"For the MFA I have to write a novel and get it faculty approved."

"When?"

"The sooner the better, I'm finished with all my credit work."

"Do you have an idea, a plot or something?"

"How about a guy joining a civil war and meeting a lovely gypsy woman?"

"Wow, you do want to be a standup comedian. I'll get the next round, okay?" She went to the bar being worked by Gisela and got two more refills of Pilsner.

"How are you supporting yourself?" I asked when she returned.

"Struggling. Some help from home. So, are you going to tell me about your novel?"

"That's the problem. I don't have a clue, no plot, nothing."

"Not a pastoral piece about Long Beach?"

"Now you're the comedian."

We stuck around for a while longer and listened to a few poets that Ralph-E. introduced. One guy, I forget his name, claimed he was a musician first and a poet second. It showed. His poetry was a confusing stream of conscious-ness with a lot of name-dropping of jazz greats from Charlie Parker to Miles Davis. It reminded me of Ferlinghetti but with much less sense. Another poet was trying to emulate Charles Bukowski, but his raw sexual imagery made me uneasy in the presence of the classy woman I had just met.

"I was talking with the big buxom lady at the bar in the traditional German peasant dress."

"That's Gisela, the other half of the ownership here with Gerhardt."

"I asked her about her getup, the same as the waitresses in the dining room. Cute, like something out of a movie. She called it a *Dirndl.*"

"Most of the girls waitressing are from the university. Gisela likes to help them out. She treats them like her daughters. They make good money on the weekends. People get loose with the tips after enough beer. You said you were struggling, where?"

"JC Penny's in the Lakewood Shopping Center."

"Oh, please! You can do better."

"Like what may I ask?"

"Well, see if Gisela can use you?"

"Waiting tables?"

"Why not.? Fewer hours with tips…and dinner thrown in, I'm told."

And that is how this story began. My new friend Pilar was hired that evening, but Gisela would be training her for her first few evenings. The restaurant drew people from all over Long Beach because the Garden had the only authentic German cuisine in town.

It was the fall semester and Pilar and I had begun a relationship, not torrid but relaxed, which helped me clear my head and focus better on my work and the problem of the novel. Pilar was able to quit the low-paying retail job at Penny's and put in a few nights every week at the Bavarian Garden to where she said she was no longer struggling. In a month, Pilar had already succeeded in charming Gisela and Gerhardt as much as she had charmed me. I cut back on my visits to the Garden because I didn't want to feel I was imposing either on Pilar or Gisela. It was still a business after all that they had to conduct. I would still go to the bimonthly poetry readings just to support Ralph E. and the poets, many who came from our English department at the University.

Christmas was fast approaching, and the Garden was doing some heavy business with the older crowd. Pilar was bright and effervescent. She was cute in her peasant *dirdl* outfit which emphasized her small waist. She was wearing her hair rolled up for the work which I thought made her look sophisticated and glamorous, her slender neck accentuated by the hair style. At the last poetry reading before the holiday, when I had ordered a mug of Pilsner at the bar from Gerhardt, we fell into a short chat.

"Your *madchen* is doing a vonderful job. Ve love her. She's good vorker,"

"Happy to hear that," I replied. "And how are you doing, Gerhardt?" I continued, not knowing what else to say.

"Munich Bayern is vinning this season," he bubbled.

"In the German league, yeah?"

"You like football, professor?"

"I played a bit of intramural soccer in my freshman year."

"Excellent! So, what position you play?"

"Midfield forward, sometimes wingman. I wasn't very good."

"Before the war, I play. Too slow, like turtle."

"I was fast, but no ball control."

"Here," Gerhardt said, sliding my filled glass toward me and lifting his own, "Ve drink to da *shön* game, ya?"

"To Pele!" I toasted, raising my glass.

"To Franz Beckenbauer!" Gerhardt responded and we drank.

I think that evening Gerhardt and I bonded beyond his deep respect for education and educators. He himself never had the opportunity to go to university in Germany, so he told me. That was reserved for rich families. He addressed me as *professor*, not understanding the distinction between *professor*, what I hoped to become and what I was, an untenured part-time instructor. Before I left the Garden an hour later, I peeked into the dining room and gave a high sign to Pilar rounding a table and putting down plates of food in front of patrons. She was strong too.

University classes came to an end in the second week of December for the Christmas holiday. There was always a round of parties to attend, also a private affair. Pilar was invited to a private party by Gerhardt and told she could bring the nice young man of hers, the professor, who they were accustomed to seeing at the Garden. Chef Otto, an older distinguished man, was invited but no other employees. It was mainly a family affair with some community friends to be held at a special private residence.

The Bixby Hill Estates was a gated community of luxurious condos and large million-dollar homes recently built within blocks of the university. Pilar and I were put on a guest list, and we would be checked in at the gate by showing our licenses. The two guards at the gate were both packing side arms.

The impressive thing about such communities was not only the obvious security with entrance guards and CCTV cameras everywhere, but the perfection with which every-thing was manicured and made sparkling. As you drove by the mansions, they were a sober reminder of the conspicu-ous wealth that existed in our midst. The upkeep alone, I guessed, had to cost more than many middle-class families made in a year. We followed the directions given at the gate, driving up a curving road until we plateaued on a broad cul-de-sac from where we could see the Pacific. We had found the location of the Christmas party. A small sign at the head of the broad driveway read *Von Frieden*. Indeed, the mansion was like the big estate homes I'd seen in England and on the continent, only smaller. The tall double doors at the entrance opened into a cavernous hallway with marble floors. We were then led with a few other guests by a servant to a tennis court sized room with a timbered high ceiling which our guide called the ballroom. Pilar and I simulta-neously exchanged astonished looks. At the far end of this space was a trio of piano, bass and guitar playing American songbook pieces mixed with a few Christmas songs. White-shirted servers with bow ties were circulating with trays, some with flutes of Champagne and others with exquisite canapes. I was not naturally paranoid, but I felt somehow uncomfortable to be invited into such opulence. My worries were allayed when we saw Gerhardt and Gisela enter the ballroom, shaking hands and convening with other guests. I stopped worrying when I realized people weren't dressed to the nines, no tuxedos or such, just average sport jackets and ties and the ladies in middle-of-the-road couture, no academy award night dresses.

About an hour later, champagne had washed away the initial intimidation we had felt, and people, maybe fifty in all, were friendly, introducing themselves and being generally gracious. Tables at one side of the ballroom had been laid with assorted large platters of savory treats from roast goose, beef, and lamb kabobs to grilled king salmon. Most people picked at these entrees and ate from small plates while standing. Many of the people we met had German surnames and almost all were old enough to be social security recipients. There were a few guests in our age group, but they were mostly stand-offish and acted embarrassed, as if they didn't want to be at the party. Pilar had been dragged off by Gisela and had joined a circle of guests. Gerhardt, now mildly drunk but functional, approached me. I was standing near the back end of the ballroom, out of the way.

"You vant to meet the man?"

"What man?"

"Von Frieden. The good Colonel Von Frieden!" There was emphasis on the title. "Dis is his house, ya?!"

The piano combo had ceased playing their soft music and then unmistakable martial music came quietly from ceiling speakers and slowly increased in volume. People began singing along in German, then more joined in until the ballroom resounded in unison. I had seen old black and white 1930s documentary films of the Nazis and their patriotic songs. As they launched into the song, I clearly caught the *Deutschland, Deutschland Uber Alles* lyrics. Gerhardt had stepped forward and raised his raised his champagne glass and joined in the singing. During this champagne fervor with everyone singing and raising glasses toward a large black, yellow, and red flag hung on the forward wall, I backed away and slipped into a low-lit hallway, hoping to find a restroom which I did after a few steps. I relieved myself and then splashed my face with cold water to sober up. Instead of going back to the ballroom, curiosity took me deeper into the house down the hallway. At the end of the hall, there were two doors, one on either side. At this point, I had the impulse to snoop just a little. The first door opened upon what looked like a dressing room with full length mirrors and closet doors, nothing intriguing. The other door opened into an office with shelves of books and a huge mahogany executive desk. Glancing back up the hall to check that I was still alone, I slipped into the office and went to the desk where I looked at the framed photos—first a young couple and two children with dress styles that seemed from the 1940s. The next photo had the same young man in a suit, standing in front of a 50s Cadillac convertible and a factory with smokestacks in the background. Seeing the remaining two photos on the other corner of the desk confirmed my growing suspicions piqued by the patriotic singing. One was a framed studio-posed shot of the same man about my age in full Nazi officer's uniform with medals, iron cross and all. In this photo he had a vertical scar down his left cheek, perhaps a souvenir of the traditional intramural swordplay at Heidelberg university, if not a war injury. A caption at the bottom of the frame read *Oberstleutnant Albert Von Frieden 1942*. The other smaller framed photo was also of him in uniform with two young soldiers in a relaxed moment, all smiling, the Eiffel Tower in the background.

I couldn't get out of that room fast enough and return to the ballroom. The singing was just ending when I entered, and I tried to smile and act as though I felt my normal self. But I was shaken. The piano combo was resuming, and Pilar was standing by the buffet tables with Gerhardt, Gisela, and an elegant, white-haired man in an expensive suit with his back to me. As I approached the group, he turned, and I flushed so much I felt a palpitation run through my chest. It was *him*, probably in his 70s, but unmistakable with that horrendous scar down his cheek. Now sober, I called on all my resources to appear natural and composed when Gerhardt introduced me as a professor at the University to the man in the desk photo. Von Frieden offered a strong hand and a warm smile.

Moments after, Pilar zoomed in on me and wanted to know where I had been. She said everyone was singing the German National anthem when I had disappeared. I was then wondering who was crazy, me, Pilar, or the whole gathering. Pilar had been filled in by Gisela. Von Frieden was a decorated Lieutenant Colonel who had survived the siege of Stalingrad in 1943, only to be taken prisoner by the Russians. It seemed counter intuitive that a former high-ranking officer of the German Wehrmacht would be a local celebrity in Long Beach. The rest of the story was that he had become a successful CEO in the Siemen's international conglomerate in the years after the war. He had passed the balance of the war in a Russian POW camp, luckily surviving, and was never accused of or tried for any crimes after Germany's surrender to the Allies.

I described to Pilar the hallway and the office with its desk photos of his old war comrades and the posed studio shot of him in full Nazi regalia. I still felt chilled, as if the image of that room and its photos had frozen themselves in my mind.

"Just having been a soldier wasn't a crime, was it?" Pilar said.

"I don't know. This whole thing is like something out of a movie."

Talking with Gerhardt moments later, I found out that Von Frieden threw a Christmas party every year for German transplants in the area.

"He vas only doing his duty as a soldier, ya? Only the fronts, no camps. He has helped many of us in this new country, including me."

"How?"

"Gisela and me vere poor ven ve came to America., no money to make business. Von Frieden lend the money to make da Garden."

"And old Otto?"

"He vas in the Russian camp vith Herr Von Frieden."

"This all sounds so incredible."

"It vas very real thirty years ago, *mein* Professor. You vere just a baby, ya?" As he said this, he put a finger across his mouth to counsel silence. "Best not to advertise." I wasn't going to say a word. I was afraid in a way I couldn't yet explain to myself.

I knew I had been out of bounds, nosing around in the rooms off that hallway. Von Frieden's past was surely not to be touted for public consumption. It was well-known that many surviving German soldiers after the war went on to become successful businessmen. But why would Von Frieden keep these Nazi mementos? He had to be proud of his past service and nostalgic about his adventurous youth. He apparently hadn't been linked to any criminal behavior. If he had been, he would have been apprehended long ago.

After the holidays, life resumed as usual—classes, Pilar, Gerhardt and Gisela, nights at the Garden. But my imagination had transported me to wild but perhaps credible suppositions. I imagined Von Frieden as part of an organized ratline for criminal Nazi fugitives in Mexico after the war, who were smuggled across the border in Siemens' trucks, given money and fake papers and hidden like needles in the haystack of greater Los Angeles.

I had a novel to write.

Mister Touchdown

ike many young men, Norman Simpson had dreamed of being famous, a writer or even a movie director. But like most, he carried on quietly in obscurity, his dreams tucked away so that they would not interfere with the path he'd chosen. After graduate school he spent two years believing in his noble path. He would lead his students into the light of Shakespeare, Yeats, T.S. Eliot ad enlightenment. But at the end of two years of teaching at Long Beach Wilson High School, he had doubts about compulsory education. He simply had a job to do. No Mr. Chips for him.

He got married after graduate school to Sandra, and now they had a child on the way. He was still the youngest member of the department's tenured faculty, but he had begun to feel as old as his associates when he found himself often engaged in empty conversations about teaching units, problem students, textbook choices, and credit union policies. His career path seemed even more predictably on rails when he found himself participating in PTA activities. His life was laid out for him.

Sandra had begun complaining about their apartment, their little *love nest* which they had lived in since they were married five years ago. She said they needed something bigger, and so they started taking the Sunday paper to read the weekly classified rental offerings. Every event that took place at home and at school was predictable. How many years of predictability was he to live through? Even the lunches his wife packed for him began to be predictable. Was this predictability the same for everyone or had his older associates become inured to it all, year after year. Was that their comfort? Shouldn't he be glad to have a steady salary and summers off and be able to see the tenured road ahead?

It was again the season for cheering, pep pins, *On Wisconsin*, school dances and Homecoming, all a heady fever wrought by the football season and the home team. For Norman, it meant his first year of tenure. But all the school spirit everywhere was blowing by him, leaving him with an unshakeable melancholy. He sat through the football rallies in the gym, wishing he'd picked up enough degree credits to qualify for coaching secondary school sports in addition to teaching English. It would have got him out of the classroom a bit. He had never been a great player in high school, but he understood the game. Had he been able to throw a football well enough, he would have gone for the quarterback position, instead of settling at halfback.

The drums and cheering now rose to a crescendo in the gym as the band played the *Notre Dame Fight Song,* while pom-pom girls, flag girls, and baton girls, all kicked, danced, and cheered. More than a decade had passed since he had been on the field of this joyous ritual, with jersey number 26 at right halfback for his high school team. He remembered the floating euphoria and deafening home crowd when he ran for one of his only two touchdowns in his senior year, a 60-yard punt return that put the team ahead in the fourth quarter. Unforgettable.

Recomposing himself, Simpson went off to teach his fifth period class, Senior English.

"Coming to the game tonight, Mr. Simpson?"

It was Ben Grady, the school prize slot back and the prize numbskull of his fifth period class. But he liked Ben. They would sometimes talk about football, certain games, plays and leagues. Since Simpson had told Ben about his high school experiences, talking football became a regular topic between them. Simpson hoped the football talk would help when he had to talk to Grady about learning to put together readable sentences.

"I'm going to try, Ben."

Simpson had no intention of attending the Friday night game. He had already made excuses for not going to the first two games of the season. His wife was agreeable if he wanted to go, but he saw his students all week long, and he didn't want to be with them in the stands on Friday night. He'd had an invitation earlier in the week from Bill Bergstrom, a senior teacher in the department, to drop over for cocktails which Simpson much preferred.

The tardy bell rang, and he checked his seating chart for absences. There were the usual deadbeats with whom he didn't concern himself. But Tina Rhys was absent. She was an outstanding student and had never been absent since the semester began. She had become, in the first month of the school year, the reason why he looked forward to fifth period. When he had started teaching, it hadn't been uncommon for him to get distracted by attractive female students, especially those that seemed more mature for their years. But he'd weathered them all and the phase passed. Tina was different from all the others. She didn't have that flippant, blasé way about her. She was unadorned simplicity, pastoral like hayfields, clear streams, pine trees illuminated by evening sun, and ground soft-quilted with moss and a bed of browned pine needles, a Celtic princess.

The class was settled and silent, awaiting him. He paused verbally, not quite remembering where to begin as he was still somewhere among his Tina inspired pines. A quick glance at his notes and he was reminded there was to be a writing assignment on Shakespeare's sonnets. The day before he had prepared them with a lecture and some analyses of samples. He outlined the writing assignment to the class again, giving them the numbers for the sonnets they could select from for analysis. As he surveyed the classroom, his eyes came back around to Tina's empty seat.

The class went to work, and he returned to his desk to make out the absence slips. Usually, he used times like this to catch up on correcting papers, but it was Friday, and he had the weekend to catch up. He finished the absence slips, and then relaxed into his swivel desk chair. He looked out through the window across the campus and into the pines that edged the parking lot. The sky was hot blue on this Indian summer day. He looked at Tina's empty seat and thought of her natural flaxen hair that fell to her shoulders. *Shall I compare thee to a summer's day....* If only he could produce some words comparable to Shakespeare's that would immortalize the quality of his feelings for her. He knew he was being foolish. But when he saw her, when she was near enough that he caught her scent, perhaps her soap, what he felt was undeniably real. Wasn't he like the lad frozen in pursuit of the girl portrayed in Keats' *Ode on a Grecian Urn*? *She cannot fade, though you hast not thy bliss.* Dismiss this infatuation, he thought. But then it *was* harmless. He had forgotten that old crazy feeling of *having fallen* until he rediscovered it in Tina. *What wild ecstasy.*

How he consciously avoided her in class as if afraid of her. Focusing his gaze on her caused his body to react, his pulse to change and his speech to struggle. He admonished himself, be still my foolish heart!

He did call on her to recite occasionally when he felt strong enough. She always gave a brief, accurate and intelligent answer, rare in these academic classes where the girls mostly stalled and ummed and aahed. Tina was clearly beyond her class.

Norman left his desk and walked down the side of the room, glancing at student work at their desks. At the back, he took a vacant desk. Some of the students who made it a habit of chatting, took peripheral glances at him, and then turned back to their papers. The class worked silently. He was picturing himself up at this desk, trying to imagine how he looked in his mobile manner of lecturing, which he had inherited from his favorite professor in his undergrad days. He wondered how he might improve his appearance with new pairs of slacks with a slimmer cut, or perhaps a new sport coat, something distinguished and professorial.

He got up from where he was sitting and walked around the back end of the room, stopping momentarily at Tina's empty seat. He glanced toward his desk again, reconsidering the angle of its position. He then went back to the front of the room and to his desk. Again, gazing at the hot blue sky and then at Tina's empty seat, he decided he would try to write a sonnet. He thought that maybe it was because she was absent that he couldn't get her off his mind. Her absence was harder to ignore than her presence. Was that a harbinger of things to come when she was graduated and gone forever? Would she live on in his reveries? Would her memory haunt him? He would have to find his love for Sandra again, which had receded with the pregnancy.

He looked down at his blank sheet of paper, jotting a few words about endless blue sky and evergreen pines as possible starting places. He was trying to capture the insurmountable distance of the beloved when he sensed a presence near him. Then he recognized Tina's scent and saw her long slender fingers handing him a tardy excuse slip. He felt his face get hot and he made an awkward attempt to cover what he had started writing.

"I was at the counseling office," she said. He acknowledged her with barely a glance.

"Very good, Tina. We're writing analyses of Shakespeare's sonnets, a short paragraph for each of the assigned, starting with number 18."

He told her to finish what she could before the end of the period. He covertly watched her go to her seat. Her walk was elegant with no sloppiness or wiggle, mature. As she sat down, she looked up, directing at him what appeared to be a grateful smile. He nodded back to her and checked her into his attendance record.

He took off his glasses and laid them on the desk. Why did his eyes have to go bad in graduate school? Maybe he ought to try getting contact lenses. He had to check his school insurance to see if they would be covered. He and Sandra had to save as much as they could with the baby coming. Perhaps he would just change the frames of his glasses for now and get some bold, executive looking frames.

When the bell rang for the end of the period and the class started filing out, leaving their papers on his desk, he asked Tina if she'd had enough time and she replied that she'd got a few of them done.

"It's the quality of the writing that matters," he declared for her and for others within ear shot.

He'd seen some of her work already during the semester and she knew how to write a sentence. That's how it was with language, some had the knack, and many didn't. Those who had read books instead of growing up with their heads in a television had a variety of vocabulary and sentence structures. It always showed.

"See you at the game, Mr. Simpson." It was Ben Grady.

"Good luck tonight, Ben." Norman said and smiled. Friday night high school football was a rite of passage that infected everyone. He had never forgotten. He was nearing thirty now, the last dozen years passing in an instant, from no cares to all the cares in the world. He remembered his father consoling and counseling him about his high school team's loss to their crosstown rival that it would seem trivial one day when he would have to face bigger challenges and responsibilities. His father had been wise. He inwardly laughed when he thought of himself telling Ben Grady a loss that night would be trivial. *Prepare yourself, Ben, to pass the college entrance exam. Try that for an end run.*

It was lunch period and Norman stayed in his home room, ate the ham sandwich Sandra had made for him and had tea from his thermos. He would make some comments on the sonnet papers rather than spending any more time on trying to write one. He went through the stack and pulled out Tina's paper:

"Sonnet #18
This is essentially a love poem, though the object of its affection is not as straightforward as it may initially seem. The poet tries to find an appropriate

metaphor to describe his beloved, suggesting that she or he might be compared to a summer's day, the sun, or "the darling buds of May." Yet as the speaker searches for a metaphor that will adequately reflect his beloved's beauty, he realizes that none will work because all imply inevitable decline and death. Where the first eight lines of the poem document the failure of poetry's traditional metaphors to capture the beloved's beauty, the final six lines argue that eternal beauty is best compared to the poem *itself*. It is this very sonnet that both reflects and preserves the beloved's beauty. So, sonnet 18 can be read as honoring not only the speaker's beloved but also the power of poetry itself, which, the poet argues, is a means to eternal life."

Norman wrote at the top of her paper, *good work, Tina. A+ With your talent, please continue with college next fall. NS*

The school day at last was finished. He had finished the papers from fifth period. He packed away remaining student papers from his other classes for correction and comment into his briefcase, tidied his desk, and then headed to the parking lot adjacent to the athletic field. The band was having a last practice in their street clothes, marching, and playing *Mr. Touchdown* which crept up his spine and tickled the hairs on his neck. As he drove out of the lot and toward home, the music narrowed and thinned and then disappeared into the hum of his car and the surrounding traffic, and he breathed deeply. He would make it through this year. Next fall would be another season, a fresh batch of students.

Sandra welcomed him home with a kiss and a cold beer. She had made a special Friday dinner of Bouillabaisse. The table was set, and a whole untouched, baguette lay waiting to be broken. The smell of saffron from the French seafood stew filled their little apartment. He felt calm for the first time all day.

"There's a good movie on TV tonight, *My Fair Lady*, ever see it? With Audrey Hepburn."

"I already know the story. Besides, she's not my type."

"Am I?" She was being coquettish.

"What do you think?" Norman replied.

"Are we going over to the Bergstrom's later?"

"How about an early night instead?"

"An early night's good."

Coupling

----

asha Barett was never my type which is perhaps why
I understood her and could be objective, even dispas-
sionate about her many problems. We'd met in little
theater while waiting to be called to the stage to read for
auditions. Sometime later in our association I learned that
her real name was Barbara Sellers, not a good stage name,
she explained. Our town's little theater was just her first stop
before she made the plunge by moving to Hollywood and
a life in Los Angeles. She'd done a lot of little theater, while
I was a just a beginner. I imagined I could play some parts
just by being myself, but I had no ambition to become a lost
soul wandering on Sunset Blvd.

She was cast in that first auditions meeting although I
wasn't, but then we wound up together in a couple succes-
sive productions after that, her acting in supporting roles
while I was getting my stage legs with walk-on bit parts.
During that time, we circled each other, both knowing there
could not be anything romantic. We got as far as coffee dates
and long rambling conversations.

A year later, auditions were announced for an obscure
piece called *After Liverpool* by British playwright James
Saunders, which our director renamed *Coupling*, hoping
to attract more interest. The play was a collection of scenes
rather than a conventional play about problem burdened

couples which especially had currency in the mid-70s when so many people were busy analyzing their love lives and their relationships. Liberation had come with the 60s, and in the wake of the 60s in the following decade came confusion and questioning.

Zasha and I were cast by director Aaron Davis, a tall, silver-haired handsome man in his fifties whose soothing baritone voice inspired confidence and affection. He told us the production would be an ensemble production which Zasha explained meant we'd be like family interacting equally. Indeed, of the four men and four women, we were to have eight short scenes, all with different pairings.

I was thrilled and frightened at realizing I was going to go on stage in a major speaking role. The director wanted us to choose wardrobe from our own according to what we thought our scenes required. Improvising became a part of the production. Director Davis was not a stickler for lines so long as you got across the lines with the same sense and the cue and didn't wander too far off script. This had a relaxing effect on all of us. He even had us in pairs improvising around situations he gave us—like, *you have come home late, and the wife is miffed because she went to some trouble to make a special dinner.* It was surprising how people came up with different interactions and levels of emotions. We did a lot of such improv sketches before we got to the play book.

For Zasha and me it was especially fun but odd to act out being a couple because we had circled each other off stage for some time with the mutual recognition and understanding that we were not going to happen. Just the right amount of warmth was retained that pulled us together. We'd tell each other about embarrassing things we'd had happen to us and it was kind of freeing. Yet sometimes the way she looked at me made me wonder if she were biding her time until I might respond romantically. So, there were times I felt I could have gone with her if I had wanted. But from those early theater days, I had other interests in the chase, mainly a heartbreaker shaped like an hourglass with auburn hair down to her waist who had taken my breath away on our first chance meeting in a cashier's queue at Quality Market.

I was thirty-four at the time, perhaps a little old for my carefree status but much too young in my head to be anywhere near settled in a marriage and all that entails. I was making a few hundred a week schlepping sandwiches to convenience stores as the Earl of Sandwich which was my business name that appeared on my plastic wrapped ham, egg salad and salami sandwiches that I made up at a rented restaurant kitchen three times a week at dawn. Not very glamorous for a guy with an advanced education and a lead in an intelligent local play production, but I was my own boss, and the money was enough to get by. At least I wasn't on the dole. I could afford a movie and a few dates, pay the rent and keep gas in my car.

Zasha was not unattractive. She had dates. She was tallish, filled-out, curvaceous, a pleasant face framed by a Sassoon haircut, a woman who would appeal to many men. I think I didn't cross the line with her because I genuinely liked her and didn't want to ruin our friendship. I couldn't pretend romantic love for the sake of satisfying a moment of lust. As I said, my inclination went in a different direction toward one Sylvie, the hourglass who possessed a waterfall of auburn hair. I was in total lust with Sylvie. I almost felt guilty about talking about her to Zasha. One of our scenes in *Coupling* was about a couple sorting out the inevitable ending of their relationship. Imagination and reality momentarily crossed paths, yet we perfected the scene, one local critic writing in a review that we managed to weave nuances around our words, strengthening the lines and forcing the audience to recognize complicity in the same games. I got a special note for my closing monologue.

We drifted apart after that show. I went on to some directing with another theater group in town and Zasha moved to Hollywood. We exchanged cards for almost a year. We used to joke a la *Casablanca* that *we'd always have Coupling.* We enjoyed our in-joke without probing the irony too much. Thereafter, we often employed lines from the play in our nostalgic back-and-forth. She claimed to have made some connections with a few luminaries such as Jamie Leigh Curtis and survived LA, although I never heard about any stage or film successes.

Meanwhile, having tired of the sandwich business and not getting very far with Sylvie, I sold the sandwich business for three grand, and I went off to Japan. After a few months of itinerant English teaching with a temp visa, I discovered one could make six figures teaching University English. So, I put together an impressive curriculum-vitae, including copies of my Californian degrees and a few commendations, and went shopping. Within a year I scored a fulltime university position with the help of a drinking acquaintance who happened to be on the faculty. A year later I met and married Marta, a lovely Japanese-German woman with whom I lived an uncomplicated decade without children while working a soft, tenured university schedule.

Zasha and I remained in contact with cards—Christmases and our birthdays in July. We wrote long compact messages in cursive on the inside blanks. Los Angeles was a huge sea for her where she was adrift, her only compass being her unflagging desire to succeed as an actor. A friendship with Jamie Leigh Curtis helped her get a SAG card and she had an agency circulating her actor's portfolio. She supported herself with everything from waitressing to childcare and acting as an au pair for rich immigrant families. At one point she had signed up for the LA wing of the old Lee Strasberg acting academy, but averred she could no longer brook the boredom. She didn't need lessons she herself could teach. She got some extra work in several features and a couple of commercials for television which relieved her of survival work. And her friendship with Jamie Leigh Curtis gave her confidence and moral support.

I celebrated her small victories in my cards, usually commented on the popular films and Broadway plays of the day, and I described my life at the university. There was a lot I could say about Marta, but in retrospect I realized I had given few details. Tri-lingual, Marta worked for Lufthansa Airlines downtown in Shinjuku. Her father had been German, and her mother Japanese, and she'd majored in English at Tokyo University. When I met her, I had thought she was way out of my league. I fell for her, and she mysteriously fell for me which has never ceased to keep me in wonder. None of this I described to Zash. I did tell her that I sometimes tired of Japanese formalities that made everyone predictable and the same, but the order and peace of the society kept me in a comfortable trance, I suppose, somewhat the opposite of Zasha's crazy environment in Hollywood where every day was dicey with chasing illusive dreams. Then a card came from Zash in which she announced getting married. Finally. She was deliriously happy with the handsome Cliff, six years her junior, who worked as a techie in the film industry. That she had made a point of his being younger told me she held some concern for this as I did. They had found an inexpensive small apartment in Santa Monica, and she was becoming domestic. This state of bliss lasted about a year until she complained in her cards that Cliff wasn't equal to her affection and desire for interaction. I was disappointed for her but not surprised. I knew about this. When I was younger, I had tired of a few women in my time. Six months later after Zasha's initial complaint, she wrote that she couldn't stay with Cliff any longer. He was indecisive, a true Libra, so she would make the move for them. She also wanted to know what work opportunities there were in Tokyo.

Marta had an old college friend running a *juku* in the Shibuya district, occupying the 8th floor of a newer highrise building, conveniently close to a metro stop. *Jukus* were small private schools that prepped students for national academic exams, but in this case the *juku* was a kind of non-academic English school (club) for adults who maintained their English as a hobby or in some cases for their professional needs in international business. These schools survived on employing entertaining native speakers of English and encouraged social gatherings among students. Zasha, having a BA in theater arts and a California resume, would fit in perfectly with her acting skills. Students would be fascinated to hear stories about Hollywood, actors, and the movies. Since there was always turnover, the demand for native English speakers never stopped and no special teaching degrees were required. I had worked in one of these social *jukus* when I first came to Tokyo. Later, of course, I was privileged and lucky to find employment at a university where my MA and several semesters of teaching at a California state university back in the 70s qualified me for the more serious task of formally teaching young people seeking degrees. Mine was a coveted position with all the benefits and cushy schedule of a university. The *jukus* were a playground by comparison and the teacher pay commensurate, in most cases, with no benefits. These schools did however provide the casual traveling American with a working visa and permission to stay in the country. By the 1990s, I found Americans teaching English in Tokyo were almost as plentiful as wannabe actors in Hollywood.

Two months after the card from Zasha announcing her final breakup with the adored but disappointing Cliff, she arrived at Narita airport with visa in hand and prepared to leave Californian dreaming behind. As I drove to the airport to pick her up, my imagined scenarios of her new life in Japan amounted to worry for her and the Japanese she would have to work for. She wasn't always easy. Japan was not a stage where you could get in the face of the director, so to speak.

Marta was completely gracious in welcoming Zasha, finding her a small apartment, a typical 400 square foot studio. Marta also vouched for her with the landlord and smoothed the transition for Zasha into the *juku* of her friend Mieko. Zasha and I had our first time together at a Denny's a week later.

"So here I am, fallen off the Cliff."

"Sooner or later, I expected you to say something like that."

"Marta is simply gorgeous, I mean, a Eurasian doll."

"What happened with Cliff?"

"It's simple, he didn't love me."

"He married you!"

"He was a very confused young man."

"Which you found out after the fact."

"He really knew nothing about love."

"He was inexperienced."

"After two years I felt very lonely."

"You needed more than he was able to give."

"His tech work was steady, but all I did was wait for phone calls."

"That didn't come."

"Precisely."

"You knew it was going to be tough to break in."

"Jamie Leigh was sweet and encouraging."

"But you ran away."

"And you got married."

"I thought it was about time."

"You men have a longer shelf life."

"Remember our play?"

"Of course, I was reminded a lot by Cliff."

"I remember my long monologue."

"Funny how we have remained friends."

I just smiled at her last comment and motioned the waitress for more coffee. Zash liked the new job at Meiko's *juku* and was assigned advanced students with whom she could have easy conversations. The advanced students were usually mature with more money which was in Mieko's interest. Her profit lay in repetitive attendance. I was happy that I could help Zash and happier that it was working out at the *juku*. If it hadn't, Marta would have had some answering to do—and then me. Zash told me she and Mieko were getting along. She had even taken Zash out for some local color, showing her the bars nearby where she knew all the proprietors. I'm glad Zash was not much of a drinker. Japan would have been a dangerous place otherwise—a nation of alcoholics in denial.

Almost a year of relative unchanged peace passed by, Marta and I took a winter holiday to Bali on comp tickets from Lufthansa and spent a week sunning on the beaches, dining and shopping. We spent our anniversary in Ubud in a thatched hut in the middle of a rice paddy in the company of nightly choruses of geckos. Ubud was like a huge box store of inexpensive exotic crafts where I bought a few little gifts for Zash. Marta and I were having dinner our next to last night in Bali at an Ubud restaurant adjacent to a serene lotus pond.

"Were you and Zasha once lovers?" she asked.

"I knew you were waiting to ask me that. The answer's *no*, never."

"She's quite an attractive woman."

"She's the only woman friend I ever had back in the States."

"But the way she looks at you sometimes?"

"Don't read anything into it. She's an actress."

"What happened with her husband?"

"She left him. A handsome guy, but boring for Zasha."

"She's not getting any younger."

"She needs constant applause."

"We all need to feel we're wanted"

"I know that but being too needy can drive a lover away."

It was true. I thought Zash dreamed of having life on a plane comparable to romantic musicals. I think at some level she wanted to be Doris Day, Natalie Wood and Barbra Streisand all wrapped into one and breaking into songs of love with a leading-type man. She was a great singer and dancer and had done some musical theater. She should have been on Broadway. One night when we all went out to one of Mieko's favorite bars, we got into singing *karoke*. The whole bar went silent when she sang the Streisand hit, *The Way We Were.*

When Marta and I got back to Tokyo, we got a call from Mieko telling us Zasha was in a bad way. She'd had a biopsy done for some breast lumps and it came out positive, diagnosing an aggressive type of cancer. Of all the worse luck after coming halfway around the world for a little work and relief from Los Angeles. Both Meiko and Marta were shaken to the depth of their womanly sensitivities and went to her aid emotionally as best they could. As for the cancer, it was classed at stage 4 and would require extensive surgery, a removal of a breast with the possibly of rebuilding with a prothesis. When the reality had a few more days to settle, I visited her and took flowers. Zasha was unnaturally upbeat and was confident that her John Roger prayers and meditation and colloidal silver would mitigate the spread. I knew about her John Roger stuff, a West Los Angeles self-appointed spiritual guru who came to prominence in the early 70s. She had also found a woo-woo English-speaking Japanese doctor who was pedaling pearl dust as a cure, but as we all knew, none of the alternatives she wanted to believe in had any effect.

She had the surgery in Tokyo, which her old parents in Grass Valley, California paid for, and once she had convalesced enough from the surgery, she would return to her family's home to recover. I visited her in post-op. An American Lutheran minister attached to the hospital had been called in and he was giving her and other ailing western patients spiritual comfort. He gave me a defeated down-cast look as he excused himself from Zash's room upon my entrance.

Zash had tears in her eyes, and I felt my face getting hot and tears forming in my eyes and then our play together all those years ago suddenly flooded my mind and I reflexively uttered, *we'll always have Coupling,* as I caressed her forehead. With effort she took my hand and brought it to her lips and gave it a light kiss. I felt the wetness of her tears on my hand, and she said, "I tried, I tried. Didn't I?"

Four months later at her home in Grass Valley, she became blind from the rampaging spread of the cancer and two months after that she died, age 38. A formal memorial card arrived from California on which her father had handwritten a few words thanking me for my kind friendship to his daughter Barbara Sellers.

The Fall of the Roman Empire

t was March of 1963 in Madrid, Spain when I got hired to work as an extra in the Samuel Bronson movie *The Fall of the Roman Empire*. Depending on the weather, I had to assemble early in the morning with several hundred other men at Atocha station where a train took us out to a broad plain that included a recreated huge set of the Capitoline Hill, the ancient center of Rome. Being capable in Spanish, I was hired to work under a couple of assistant directors who spoke no Spanish, whereas I could communicate with the Spanish extras who didn't understand English. That spring, the production of the huge sword and sandal movie paid my rent and meals. It didn't seem to matter that I didn't have a working visa in Spain, but because I was an American and they could use me I got a pass. Being an extra is like being a flagger on a road construction job, a lot of standing around and waiting. It's boring most of the time on set, until someone with a bullhorn makes the call to assemble for takes. During those weeks of the shoot, I felt glad that it was all an act and that I hadn't lived in those times. The soldier's costume and gear were uncomfortable and heavy, and the Roman style leather sandals I was issued rubbed blisters on my feet.

It was my year off from undergraduate study and the degree. Money saved, some help from family and what I could make along the way kept me afloat. Spain was dirt cheap in those days, a dollar a day for bed and board at my pension, and so I had enough. I would leave for England in the summer, where I had a job waiting for me at the Birmingham Dunlop Tire factory, arranged for me by Percy Wescott my dad's old chum from *his* traveling days from 1938-45, and I would have a free room with my grandmother Doris until September when I had to get back to start the fall term at UCLA.

Meanwhile my life in Madrid was full. Evening meals served by Josi, the pension cook and housekeeper, had taken some getting used to—like *arroz con tinta de calamari,* rice with gravy made of squid ink and *callos Madrileno,* chunks of tripe cut like ravioli squares and simmered in a spicy tomato sauce. Near Quevedo metro station a half dozen stops from city center, La Puerta del Sol, my pension was convenient as well as clean and comfortable. I shared a large room with an engineering student named Ramon Valdez whom I rarely saw, except at day's end or in the morning if I mustered for breakfast, always Spanish bread with butter and sugar and a big mug of milky coffee. The pension had been a family home at one time but now all the rooms were inhabited by separate renters, two bathrooms being communal. Down the hall there was a Cuban couple, escapees from the Castro revolution, then Felipe Solis, the hair salon *peluquero* and lastly a bullfighter from Mexico, currently campaigning in Spain. A room adjoining the kitchen was Josi's quarters.

I don't think I realized how wonderful the pension was until I got back home. How much do we appreciate moments while we're in them? I knew my days in Spain would soon end, and I'd find myself on a factory floor nine to five and then in the fall be hustling from class to class across the UCLA quad. Being young as I was, I nevertheless got bored occasionally, and so *The Fall* was a good diversion as well as providing a little income.

Around midday of a shoot in March, I spotted a cute blonde extra among the Roman common crowd who lined the way for takes of Roman celebratory victories with cheering and the throwing of flowers at the troops. The women were mostly wrapped in colorful sheet-like costumes like the togas worn by the men. I got in a lunch line behind her one afternoon and struck up a conversation. Like me, Peggy Bennett, was halfway toward a college degree, at the University of Tennessee, spoke a little Spanish and was traveling. There weren't a lot of blond women around for hire as extras, even though they wanted the crowd to look diverse. The director apparently also wanted some pretty faces in the crowd to add some glamor to the glory that was Rome. Peggy and I were both extras with a little something extra.

At the time, I had an on-and-off Spanish girlfriend, who was a great help in practicing my Spanish, but I wasn't in love with her. I wanted to have sex with her, but that was impossible in the Spanish mores of the time. I surely wasn't interested in marriage, which was pretty much one of the only avenues left open to a Spanish peasant girl in those days. I was only 22, an American male with a future. I still hadn't declared a major, never mind knowing what to do after graduation. My travel year was supposed to be my time to sort myself out. The Spanish girlfriend Blanca was a dark looker from Caceres, with that young Sophie Loren look, then having come to the big city, living with relatives, and working fulltime at the Cuba Sol coffee shop at the Plaza Cibeles. I began to feel like a cad, and I was tiring of frustrating necking sessions in Retiro Park. Finally, I just stopped calling her and dropping in at the Cuba Sol. Anyway, I had fallen in love with another woman.

By April the forces of Emperor Marcus Aurelius in the movie were on the march, I among them, and I had fallen hard for Peggy Bennett. We were both reading Lawrence Durrell's Alexandrian Quartet, then popular and a hailed investigation of modern love in four interwoven novels. They were a counterpoint to my chaste affair with Peggy. The novels were the first serious books I had read since the *Red Badge of Courage* and the *Great Gatsby* in high school which had left no special impression on me at the time. I think that Durrell's quartet with its longings, disappointments, betrayals, and intrigue lent Peggy and me a sense of sophistication when we theorized about the characters and discussed the book in general—while part of me imagined myself in my own novel with Peggy, and Madrid my Alexandria.

We were drinking wine at the Meson de la Guitarra near La Plaza Mayor one Friday night, talking about our school plans, *The Fall of the Roman Empire* and other movies, her life in Nashville and mine in LA.

"I'll never forget this little hole in the wall," Peggy said. It was a cave of a place, the plaster walls covered with inscriptions left by other drinkers, visitors, and lovers.

"Let's leave our initials and the date," she suggested. We didn't have a pencil or pen, so I inscribed our initials with the point of a suitcase key I had on a ring with others, and she rubbed some of her mascara into the engraving.

"There, that should last for a while."

"I hope forever," I said.

In May, Miguel Cruz, pension co- resident my age, got gored in his first novillada of the season in Valladolid. It wasn't grave but it did land him in the Madrid Sanatorio for bullfighters. I took him a small basket of fruit including some Canary Island blood oranges.

"So, when are they going to let you out." *Cuando te dejan salir*? After six months of speaking Spanish daily, I was becoming fluent.

"Another three days. It was only a small *cornada* about 10 centimeters," he said, pointing a finger at his thigh under the sheet. He was delighted to see me and asked about my work on the movie. I made a stiff soldierly pose and thumped my chest with my fist in the Roman soldier salute. This amused him.

"When are you going to fight again?" I queried.

"I have a date in two weeks at San Sebastian de los Reyes."

I knew the ring, a short bus ride to a village outside Madrid, a testing ground for young aspirant bullfighters. He offered me two tickets with which I thought I would take Peggy if she wasn't busy. I had no first dibs on her time. We were not engaged in any way. She may not have even liked the bullfights. I was not a raving aficionado like so many of the Spaniards, but I knew more after reading Hemingway's *Death in the Afternoon*. Becoming better acquainted with Miguel inspired my further interest, and his deep commitment to his art amazed me.

Ricardo Morales and Inez from Cuba were especially interesting tenants of the pension. They had arrived from Cuba just a year before me. They had attended Havana University in the same class as Fidel Castro. Apparently, he was even a leader in his college days and had graduated at the head of his class. They had a friendly relationship with him that continued a year or so after the overthrow of the dictator Baptista, but then Castro began to infringe on the news and reporting in which both Inez and Ricardo were employed. Castro had begun tailoring news and reports to fit his agenda. Any opposition was quickly persecuted. One morning, Ricardo and wife Inez didn't show up at the TV broadcasting station because they had been smuggled out of the country on a Panamanian freighter bound for Spain.

"Why Spain?" I asked in English. Both he and Inez spoke fluent English and had spent many a holiday in Florida back in the day.

"Good question. We have a lot of relatives in Spain, but we are no longer journalists. That was a provision of our immigration and getting our residence. The General doesn't really want our kind in Spain, but he hates communists like Castro more than anything."

They had escaped one extreme to another. I wasn't much aware of politics at the time. I wasn't aware of Franco other than the periodic radio interruptions with military music and cheers of "Viva Franco, viva El Caudillo!" Political awareness awaited me later when I resumed college life through the latter half of the sixties.

I agreed to have a drink with Ricardo, and he poured out a couple glasses of *tinto,* the red wine purchased in bulk at the bodega.

"To President Kennedy!" he toasted JFK.

By the end of May, shooting events in the *Fall* had Marcus Aurelius dying and his crazy son Commodus succeeding him as the new emperor, and I and many others were switched from our centurion garb to shabby tunics to participate as cheering plebes at gladiatorial contests in the Coliseum, the favorite entertainment of the new emperor.

Peggy was available to go to San Sebastian de los Reyes to see my friend Miguel, now recovered, in his second novillada of the season. In preparation, I visited Felipe's *peluqueria* near the Plaza Santana downtown. He had three other barbers busy at work in the shop, shaving faces and razor cutting hair. I wanted to look my best for my date with Peggy, and Felipe literally gave me all the trimmings, including a straight razor shave, the closest I've ever had. The best part was his not charging me a peseta. When I insisted, he was adamant, "Ni una peseta, Chico!" Later that week I brought him a box of *turron*, a popular confection made of honey and almonds.

It was Peggy's first time at the bullfights, and so I explained what I knew from my recent reading of Hemingway. Miguel was stunning in his chocolate and gold suit. The bulls were bigger than I had expected with fearfully wide horns. Both Peggy and I were on the edge of our seats. All the young men performed well, including Miguel. We had a fright when he got caught and tossed without sustaining an injury, and he returned to fight closely and slowly, finishing with a sword thrust to the hilt, taking the bull down quickly. He was only awarded an ear. The judges were too conservative, I thought. He should have been awarded two. But then I was partial to my friend. He was beautiful.

Fright and excitement had put some pronounced color into Peggy's cheeks, and she was happy to share some churros just outside the ring at the conclusion of the afternoon. Before we caught the bus for Madrid, we got to see Miguel and he autographed a program for her.

With the arrival of June, shooting of the *Fall* was winding down with a lot of battle shots of the ensuing civil wars between Commodus played by Christopher Plummer, and his alienated commander Livius, played by Stephen Boyd. I simply didn't show up for the early assembly and transport to the huge set in the suburbs. That was one's effective notice. I was scheduled to be in England by the middle of June. Peggy didn't even last that long. She went off to Italy shortly after the bullfight, without too much ceremony. I had already resigned myself to the facts that she had her own path to follow, and I had mine. She was the first great heartache in my life.

There was a party at the pension for my *despedida,* my farewell. There were hearty hugs among us all, and an exchanging of addresses, and lots of wine. Josi was even smiling for a change and had made some wonderful *tapas* for the occasion. I was especially sad to say goodbye to Ramon. I had become accustomed to our many late-night Spanish conversations in the dark before falling asleep. I would never forget him.

Fast forward fifty years and my wife Joyce and I are on a Spanish holiday, spending a few days in Madrid, and we have just come up to street level at Quevedo Metro station, my old neighborhood. It is midday, and it is not unlike a busy intersection in West Los Angeles, lots of cars but more foot traffic. There are no candy and tobacco vendors from whom I used to buy a one-peseta Celta cigarette, no *bocadillo* carts selling 5-peseta calamari sandwiches, no blind lottery sellers shilling their wares, no Guardia Civil in a patent leather tricornia hat, suspiciously eyeing everyone. Strolling south on Fuencarral boulevard toward Calle Olid, I note the buildings have been refreshed with new facades, few remaining with ornate iron balconies. Number 3 Olid, my old address, has a new portal and iron gate where I remember late nights and clapping for the *portero* to come running with his jangle of keys to open the iron gate. Back out on Fuencarral, where there had been a bodega and a couple tavernas is now dotted with specialty shops and a women's boutique. There were so few women in the streets back in the old days and never in the bright styles now seen. Most wore black, as if women were forever in mourning. We are now in front of the boutique featuring women fashions. Joyce is brightened and wants to look inside. She is sorting through skirts and dresses hung in rows along a wall. The salesgirls study her. I start to take a seat when a large reddish cockroach scurries out from hiding and pauses. I reflexively shoot out a foot and squash it in an instant which earns me a tart "Bravo!" from one of the salesgirls who glares at me with a sharp look of contempt. *A Spanish Buddhist?!*

It is only the end of April but already the temperature is climbing. I want to find a cool place to sit and take a little refreshment. I decide to take us back to Plaza Santa Ana downtown, only a short metro ride from Quevedo. The Plaza Santa Ana is still the lovely little square with trees and benches I had frequented during my youth. It is also the location of the Cerveceria Alemania, a quaint old bar with an interior intact from the turn of the century where I often had a tap beer and mussels in garlic sauce. So, my wife and I step into the Alemania, now air-conditioned, and we find a quiet place near a wall with several old action photos of Luis Miguel Dominguin, one of Spain's legendary mid-century bullfighters. I'm not sure, but the photos look familiar. We order glasses of cold tap beer and a plate of mussels. Joyce is happy to cool off and she goes to the women's restroom to freshen up. Alone momentarily with my reveries, I go back to a day in the Cerveceria when I'd bought a gold ring from a sharpie at the bar. He claimed it was a diamond and to prove it he scratched a nearby window with it. Young naive mark that I was, thinking the ring was cheap because it was hot, I bought it and wore it for a week until the metal of the ring began turning my finger black. The Alemania is our last stop, I think. Joyce and I have done the best of old town Madrid—La Plaza Mayor, Las Cuevas de Luis Candelas, El Botin, and of course, La Meson de la Guitarra where Peggy's and my wall inscription was not to be found.

"What do you say we get in some beach time in Malaga?" I suggest when Joyce returns from the restroom.

"Ah, yes, great. I really want to see the Picasso Museum."

"You bet."

The following day as our train pulls out of Atocha station bound for Malaga, I am happy to be going somewhere new. I'd never got to the south in the old days. I look forward to the beach, the sea air and the intense clear blue of the Mediterranean.

In The Year of the Pandemic

The Covid pandemic of 2020-21 changed everything. I think it was actress Shirley MacLaine who said, *while we're busy making plans, life happens.* The pandemic certainly put the brakes on most people's plans. A lot of people I thought were friends just disappeared. One beloved friend died in an accident; another got the virus and died in hospital. Our weekend dancing event was cancelled indefinitely. Our season tickets to our community theater were all cancelled. My wife Muriel and I celebrated a quiet 40th wedding anniversary in the year of the pandemic, and we finally got around to making a will. We also bought burial plots next to each other with simple headstones. I would have been fine with cremation, but my wife wanted our bio-degradable burial side by side. It won't make any difference, will it? I will most likely be the first to be planted since I'm twelve years older than she is. We still have to fill out forms and register them with the cemetery about what we want engraved on our headstones, last words, if you like.

The pandemic has been a season to take stock. I suspect it has many of us seniors refocused on our mortality. Equally sobering for me is a nearby homeless encampment of about four acres of ragtag tents, a replay of the Great Depression. I feel at once sad and yet thankful that I am not one of them. Not all the homeless are young and durable. I always see a few white-haired individuals in the encampment. I do know a little bit about it. When I hit the road with Jack Kerouac optimism back in the 60s, I slept rough enough times to never want to repeat the experience. In those days it was an adventure; now it has become a forced way of life for a huge population of displaced poor people, grown larger by the pandemic.

Because I keep an active email account, I can't help seeing the lead stories of the day that come up after I close out my mail. And so, I am aware of what's trending. The so-called millennials, people in their 30s, are said to be economically stunted, that they will never acquire the economic levels reached by their parents. Why is that? I often read this is the *gig economy* where people work two and three part time jobs to make ends meet. I sympathize with these young people. I struggled in the economy for two decades before they were born, which is why I luckily got out by going abroad. Economic security in America is a mirage unless you are among the few who are lucky enough to have become rich. Social Security is not much of a safety net. And we all know sickness can financially ruin us, which shouldn't be the case in an evolved nation.

I personally know Boomers who struggle, especially women who didn't have careers and made failed marriages. They are now old, alone and living hand to mouth. Then there are the Vietnam veterans. There are far too many who fell through the cracks and probably number more than a few at my neighborhood homeless encampment.

I have lived eighty years and as I look around, I sense that all has changed for the worse, best exemplified by the hugely diminished numbers on the planet's health for which my generation is somewhat responsible. I have only to remember driving around when all we had was leaded gas. The earth has reached its tipping point, the poles are melting, species declining, weather patterns gone extreme, and now a virus pandemic rages around the world. Has the apocalypse arrived?

Some Pollyanna seniors will say, we've always had strife and wars and that's the way of the world and mankind, as if what we see now is just more of the same old, same old and can't be helped. (*Drink your beer and shut up*) Can we afford such an attitude? I remember having so much hope in the 60s, the whole Kennedy, MLK inspired era; but no, the peace couldn't be sustained. Rather than build a better America, we made more war on foreign soil, and the monied interests of America made war on the working class. Don't believe the towering DOW numbers. Look at the homeless camps and go out and talk to people who toil daily with little hope of reaching daylight at the end of the tunnel.

I'm old enough to remember impressions of Nazi bombings where I lived in Birmingham, England as a small child, and I feel as though I have known continuous war ever since. After Vietnam, we heard the mantra, *never again*. But it was empty rhetoric from our leaders and ministers. The recent Afghanistan debacle was their blundering repeat of Vietnam. Now something even bigger than their wars is upon us—a dying planet.

Lake Mead is at half-mast and threatens the water supply of 40 million people in the West. Same old same old? Smoke from massive fires and streaks of 100-plus-degree weather suffocate the western states while floods drown swaths of the USA, Europe, and China. The planet faces emergency. But in this country, taking immediate action is always trumped by finding consensus and resolve to do so. President Biden, in a latter-day effort to lift a nation in need of lifting with another New Deal, including proposals to fight global warming, is stonewalled by an opposing party with questionable, if not foolish motives. So, because the living world needs all the help and wishes it can get, I should engrave on my headstone GOOD LUCK!

I am getting my house in order. The one issue I will probably leave unsettled because I have no power to do otherwise is our daughter Yvette. Nothing is more stupid and final than the total estrangement she resolutely practices toward us as if it were virtue. We had twenty-five good years with her until she took on a spouse who we are certain made Yvette choose between her or us. Such severity was unwarranted and needless. Why else was Yvette so painfully conflicted and fraught when she announced her intention to permanently part from us? When we recently chose our burial spot, I admit I projected myself into my daughter looking at our plot when my wife and I are buried there. It's a lovely place on a slight grassy incline in the shade of a tree. I imagined her coming and looking one day when her hardness softens and her heart opens, albeit too late. But then, maybe she will pass to her own end without regret. Foolish girl.

I will never forget my 50th high school reunion. It was uplifting to find so many old classmates not fossilized by time. They were happy for the occasion, which is why such events are held. But a few poor souls had been destroyed by time. They had become embittered, and bile is all they had to offer, like my old confidant through my last two pivotal years of high school, sweet Mary Bullock. The scant back story I picked up from a couple of classmates was that she had become filthy rich through marriage and lived in the exclusive Holmby Hills district of West Los Angeles. Sadly, there was not an ounce left of the sweet, happy girl I had once known. She bitterly mocked the innocence we had all embodied fifty years ago. So, for her and my daughter and the many emotionally messed up people who wander the land, maybe I'll put on my headstone, GET OVER IT!

I don't imagine many will visit my grave, but the poet in one or two may cause them to drop by and utter a few words, a bit of self-conscious theater, as if playing in a Bogart movie, or in imitating Thomas Gray the English poet of *Elegy Written in a Country Churchyard.*

Chris Healey is a practicing poet and so he might visit if he's still above ground and in town after I'm gone. He certainly followed me through life. We knew each other in college through graduate school during the 60s as English majors, drinkers, and wannabe writers. In the decades after I moved from the LA area, our connection became distant like the 60s on which it was based. I always thought of him in a brotherly way but then Chris began periodically showing up at my changing locations from Santa Barbara to San Francisco to Oregon like an Inspector Javert on the trail of Jean Valjean. With those surprise visits, I began to sense a hint of mocking from him which would become revealed around the turn of the millennium when he completely ignored my first published book of fiction and never acknowledged it.

He received my book because I sent it certified and got his signed receipt. Chris could have sent a few words of acknowledgement, if not a critique. Our old creative writing professor Dr. John Hermann often reminded us of the Latin maxim, *de gustibus non est diputandum*, there's no accounting for taste, so that we'd remember we couldn't please everybody with our work. Fine, if Healy didn't like the book, he could have at least acknowledged publication.

It felt easier to just let the issue slide rather than call him on his disregard. I'd had enough accolades from a variety of qualified readers to know the work had merit. His disregard proved his arrogance and contempt.

By the time we were both into our 70s, Chris had the temerity to include me in his long emailing list to whom he periodically sent out his pretentious Beat-style poems, reminding me of what we liked as college sophomores, narratives chock full of esoterica and complaint, now dated like bell bottoms and lava lamps. Rather than enjoyable to read, his poems mostly strained to impress the reader with their obscure erudition. I have never seen the value in creating puzzling stories and poems, unless one is writing whodunits. I received about a dozen or so of these Beat-like poems during the year of the Pandemic, and although he solicited comments, I sent none. I expect he got the message because the poems have now ceased coming, and I hope we are finally at an end to our decades-long pretense of friendship.

I'd also like my headstone to speak to Daniel Gershom who was a kind, solicitous fellow, younger than I. He lives in town and will most likely survive me and might show up at my grave site if he has a nostalgic moment. Daniel was extraordinarily bright but needy and not blessed with physical attractiveness to women, and so he was often at a disadvantage (or just deluded) as he sought his way out of loneliness by pursuing beautiful women out of his league who ended up merely using him. Dan had been a kind friend and a good business partner until there was a conflict over an exceptionally attractive real estate agent he fancied. We had a thriving real estate partnership until he became infatuated with this female neophyte to the business whom he brought into the office. Just a few months out of real estate school, she had a couple of big listings registered in the real estate multiple listing book which I realized had to have been engineered by Dan. Both listings, I remembered, were properties he'd been courting and had mentioned several weeks earlier. This was a breach of our partnership behind my back. I confronted him, and he responded by ending our partnership. Just like that.

In the weeks that followed, the young woman, suddenly a chic business dresser, continued to show new listings in the multiple listing book under the heading of Gershom's brokerage. She was young but not innocent, and I suspected she'd play Dan for as long as she could. Dan's desperation must have been obvious to her like a big fish on light tackle. So, for Dan Gershom and Chris Healey and others in need of reminding, perhaps I should put LOYALTY on my stone or maybe SINCERITY.

To the other two women who figured prominently in my life besides my wife Muriel of 40 years, I might want to leave a special epitaph. My first wife Vicki, when I was young and in graduate school, may visit my grave with genuine feelings of loss. She was a kind-spirited, good woman. We simply hadn't had timing on our side when we got together in the 60s. We separated a few short years after marrying because we both recognized we couldn't work out in the long run. She has visited me and my wife a few times over the years and my wife has had no objection. She liked Vicki, while I kept in touch with her with birthday and Christmas cards. Her second marriage was a disaster, but at least she was left with a good daughter. Nevertheless, Vicki now in her 70s still has to work. Being sentimental like me, I envision

Vicki visiting my grave site and even bringing a modest bouquet of flowers. The thought of that possible scenario makes me feel like Burt Reynolds in the movie *The Man Who Loved Women.*

Celeste might come, likely not for any grief but to satisfy some perverse sense of justice or gloating. We weren't married but we were together in an off-and-on tumultuous relationship for almost seven years in the 70s, which hung on by a slim thread of communication into the 2000s when she started quibbling about money, which she claimed I owed her from our dealings 35 years ago. I have always felt a certain sorrow for her that she was so pecuniary and became even more so over the years. Ironically, her only child married a wealthy, disagreeable older man, money probably being the deciding consideration fostered by Celeste. Maybe I should put a good Beatle song title on my stone for Vicki and Celeste and others for whom the cap fits: ALL YOU NEED IS LOVE or perhaps better, just an ambiguous BECAUSE.

For my contemporary acquaintances and few friends, I will just have my wife let them know about my memorial, preferably in a late afternoon if in the winter, or at 8 pm in the summer, both times close to dusk. I want some music that will allow the guests to share what musical sentiments moved me in life. Some distraction would be pleasant anyway to balance the usual hyperbolic testaments of memorials. Some *O Mio Babbino Caro* and *Nessun Dorma* and perhaps Bocelli-Brightman singing *Con Te Partiro'* will put the attendees in an agreeable mood. Perhaps my wife will throw a small wake at the house with one of her great soups, crusty rye bread and a few bottles of Argentine Malbec.

But as for the engraving on the stone, I really need something that's an all-around challenge. I have never forgotten what young Hemingway's Parisian mentor Gertrude Stein had said when she lay dying, which was passed on to us by her lifelong partner Alice B. Toklas. When Gertrude asked, *What's the answer?* and got no response from Alice, she said, *in that case,* WHAT IS THE QUESTION?

I'll think about it.

Made in the USA
Middletown, DE
16 February 2022

61338065R00096